Nuisance

Nuisance

FREDERICKA BERGER

William Morrow and Company
New York 1983

Printed in the United States of America.

10 9 8 7 6 5 4 3 2 1

Library of Congress Cataloging in Publication Data
Berger Fredericka.   Nuisance.
Summary: With the help of some new friends, a teenager begins to change her
self-image, that of a nuisance to her divorced parents and stepfather.
[1. Divorce--Fiction. 2. Self-perception--Fiction] I. Title.
PZ7.B4515Nu   1983   [Fic]   82-20848
ISBN 0-688-01738-X

TO TANTE

Contents

Mr. Hawkins Is a Nerd!

Julie gazed out at the gray afternoon sky and shivered. Was it because it looked so cold outside or was it because she was nervous about her talk with Mrs. Barker? A kid came out of her office and the last one ahead of Julie got up and went in. Where had she seen him? she wondered. He wasn't in any of her classes. She sat down in his seat—a wooden, straight-backed chair. It was still warm from his having sat in it. In fact people had been sitting in it all afternoon waiting for their interviews with Mrs. Barker. At least she wasn't different from anyone else. All of the students in this school had interviews with their guidance counselors about their reports. Not like her old school, where the report was mailed home and her mother saw it before she did.

"Then what?" Julie had asked the girl who was sitting next to her in homeroom. She wasn't sure, but she thought her name was Mary.

"Then you're supposed to take it home to your parents," said Mary with emphasis on the *supposed,* which suggested that sometimes her report didn't arrive home.

"And if you don't," Julie asked, "does anyone know?" She didn't imagine that Mary's report was anything to brag about. At least if she studied, she did it without taking books home with her—only her huge purse in which rattled countless tubes and boxes of makeup.

"I keep it in here"—Mary patted the purse—"until they ask for it." Julie could picture a brown envelope covered with smudges of rouge and eye shadow. "By the time they remember, if they do, it's a month later."

"Don't they have to sign it?" Julie asked. "And aren't they angry about your not giving it to them, or about . . . ?" She didn't want to assume that Mary got bad grades. At least she never had to worry about showing anyone her report. The lowest grade she had ever gotten was a B-minus.

"Not here. Once you get your report, it's between you and your parents. And it works out. When they ask to see it, even if the grades don't look so great, I tell them I'm doing better already. 'I can handle it,' I tell them."

"And they don't bother you?"

"No, they're too busy."

The wooden chair began to feel cold and hard while Julie waited for her turn. If she didn't have to worry, Julie wondered, looking out again at the gray sky, why was she still shivering?

"Hey, you're next." The kid who'd just gone in was back already. He was holding a notebook and several textbooks and a brown envelope that had to be his report and a calculator and several pencils. He looked angry.

Because he thought he should have gotten an A instead of an A-minus, Julie surmised. He had a studious frown.

"Don't say I didn't warn you," he grumbled as Julie picked up her books.

"About what?" she asked before she left.

"Hawkins," he said and walked off. That was where she'd seen him, coming out of the advanced ninth-grade math class when she went in for regular seventh-grade math. Hawkins. They had the same math teacher. Maybe she should worry after all, quickly, just in case, before she got her report.

"Hello, Julie. Nice to see you." Mrs. Barker was writing something on a memo sheet, but she stood up smiling and holding out her hand.

It's as though I'm the one person she's been waiting to see all day, thought Julie. But it can't be real. It's the way guidance counselors are. Even if they see a hundred students an hour.

"Have a seat, and I'll be with you in a minute." Mrs. Barker went back to writing on her memo sheet. It was a relief to sit quietly for a minute and try to relax. Julie looked across at Mrs. Barker, bent over her writing. She might be somebody's grandmother with her gray hair in a knot at the back of her head. The kind of person you were supposed to tell everything to if you needed help. But Julie didn't need help. She'd always been able to manage everything by herself. Even her parents' divorce.

"Let's see," said Mrs. Barker, putting aside the memo and opening a folder in front of her. "You were thirteen . . . when?" That was to give Julie a chance to talk.

"December," said Julie.

"Did you move before or after your birthday?"

"After," said Julie. "After Christmas."

"So you've been with us for a month."

"Yes," said Julie.

"And how's it going?" Mrs. Barker reached for a brown envelope like the one the kid before her had.

"All right," said Julie.

"You're sure?" Mrs. Barker looked as though she really was concerned. "Any problems I can help you with?" Julie shook her head. "None? None at all?" Mrs. Barker drew out the words. She seemed to be giving Julie time to think of how to express herself. But it was true. The problems at school were just a part of starting a new school in the middle of the year —not knowing people and having the work be different. And the problems at home—she wasn't going to talk about them. Even if Mrs. Barker knew that her mother was divorced and that now Julie had a stepfather. Guidance counselors always knew those things.

Julie expected Mrs. Barker to say something more, but she waited. Well, if she wanted to give Julie time to confide, she could keep on waiting. "No problems, really," Julie answered, but her voice didn't sound convincing.

"I just wondered . . . ." Mrs. Barker waited again.

She probably does know everything, Julie thought. In a way, she wished she did. Then she'd have someone to talk to, because she couldn't talk to her mother anymore. Even though she'd only been married to Stephen for a month, she already seemed hard to reach. Once Stephen had started living with them, he'd grown up around her mother like a high, thick hedge.

"I wondered," Mrs. Barker said, "whether you were

aware of any difficulties with your schoolwork." She took a handful of pale green memo sheets out of the brown envelope and looked through them. "Of course grades after one month don't mean much. Teachers give them so you're sure to get credit for the semester. Altogether, you've done . . ."

My report! Why doesn't she give it to me? Julie chafed, trying to guess from Mrs. Barker's face what was on the sheets of paper.

"All your teachers seem to think you've made a good adjustment," she said, handing the papers across to Julie, "and I wouldn't be too concerned about the math." She smiled reassuringly.

Was her hand shaking as she took the papers? Her cold hand brushed Mrs. Barker's warm one. Was she going to have to read them over with Mrs. Barker sitting there watching her?

"Have a look," said Mrs. Barker. Yes, she was. "Take your time."

English, B-plus. "Julie seems to write clearly and she gets her work done on time." Yes, Julie's hand definitely shook as she slipped the first sheet to the back of the pile. History, B. No comment. Science, B-minus. "Julie's work is satisfactory and I expect she'll do even better second semester." B-plus, B, B-minus. Would the next be math, C-plus? Julie held her breath and looked. French, A-minus. "Julie has a gift for languages." That was because she'd already learned the *passé composé* in Virginia. But no matter. An A-minus was very nice. She smiled up at Mrs. Barker. Mrs. Barker smiled back and said, "Remember, though, about the math . . . ."

Julie looked down at the last sheet. Math, C-minus.

C-minus! Julie had never seen a C-minus before on anything—papers, tests. Oh, yes, on one stupid spelling quiz in sixth grade that she forgot to study for. C-minus! She looked down at the paper again. Yes. That was what it said.

"Did you read the comment, Julie?" Mrs. Barker's voice seemed to come from a distance, as though Julie had been knocked on the head and was recovering consciousness. "It's not as bad as it looks, you know. Isn't that what he says?"

"Julie's grade only reflects her test scores on work she was not familiar with," Julie read. And then, "I'm sure with some special help, her work will improve." Julie knew the pain in her eyes showed when she looked up at Mrs. Barker.

"Don't let it upset you, Julie," she said. "It's from changing schools in the middle of the year."

And from having my mom marry Stephen. That was the real cause. There was no escaping it.

"You might talk to your parents . . . ." It sounded almost like a question. As though Mrs. Barker wanted to know whether she would or could talk to her parents. But Julie didn't say anything. "About having a tutor," she continued. "Sometimes the math teachers do it after school. But it costs money. Or some of the ninth graders who are good at math like to do it for fun during study halls."

Fun for them, maybe, but not for me, thought Julie, handing the papers back to Mrs. Barker. She stood up. She wanted to leave while she was still numb, before she started feeling what it was like to get a C-minus in math. And in a new school, especially, when she wanted to make a good impression.

"You'll let me know what you decide to do," said Mrs. Barker, putting the papers in the brown envelope and handing it to her. "You can talk it over with your parents after they've seen these."

"Okay," said Julie.

"The French is wonderful," Mrs. Barker persisted. "You should be proud."

"Yeah," said Julie. She'd forgotten about the French.

"I'm always here if you want to talk." Mrs. Barker came around the desk and put her hand on Julie's shoulder. She was being very kind, but did she mean it? No matter. She knows, Julie thought. She knows how hard it's going to be for me to tell Mom and Stephen. And there was some comfort in the thought, even if nothing was said between them, even if Mrs. Barker only knew in an antiseptic, professional way. She moved toward the door and Julie left.

"See you tomorrow," she called after her, but Julie didn't answer.

"Am I going to cry?" she asked herself as she walked down the hall. "If I am, I'd better hide in the girls' room." She decided she wasn't. It was too hard and cold and awful to cry about. That's what the gray sky outside meant. Not snow, but a C-minus in math.

Most of the kids had left school already. She wouldn't meet anyone who would see the brown envelope and say, "How'd you do?" No one really knew her well enough, anyhow. In Virginia, everyone would have been asking. Lucky thing. Because she wouldn't want to tell anyone. Not even Wendy, her best friend back in Virginia.

I can't get out of this place fast enough, she thought

as she opened her locker. She wanted to stuff all her books in, take her jacket, slam the door, and never come back. Instead, from habit, she stood in front of the locker checking to see which books she could leave and which books she would need in order to prepare for the next day. All the time, she felt the heavy weight inside of her of the awful, irreversible thing that had happened—a C-minus in math.

"He's a nerd, isn't he?" a voice behind her said. "Math twenty-four hours a day. That's what he expects." It was the kid who had seen Mrs. Barker ahead of her. "Did Hawkins mess you up too?" he asked. Was this kid pretending not to know about her C-minus when he really did? But how? Had he been listening outside the office? She turned, ready with explanations about having changed schools and different work and—"Well?" he said, but he didn't wait for Julie to answer. If he didn't already know, he knew when he saw her face. "Don't let it bother you," he said, "the way I'm not going to let it get to me." He left abruptly and walked on down the hall. At least someone else has problems, thought Julie as she watched him walk, shoulders jerking and head down.

Julie pulled out the books she needed for homework. Then she held up the brown envelope. What to do with the vile creature? Not leave it in her locker. Someone might spot it and ask embarrassing questions. The trash can with the swinging lid on top? Julie was shocked at herself. She put the envelope at the bottom of her tote bag and all the other books on top so that no one could see it, zipped up her jacket, and left. At the door, she saw Mrs. Barker coming down the other hall toward her.

Does she want me? Julie paused. Has she come to say it was all a mistake? But Mrs. Barker waved and said, "Stay warm." Julie pushed open the front door and stepped out into the cold. She walked quickly. After a few minutes she pulled up her hood. If only it would snow. Julie looked hopefully at the lowering sky. If it snowed, she wouldn't have a math class tomorrow and maybe the next day. And she could put off telling Mrs. Barker whether she wanted a tutor and she could put off— That was the big problem. When, to whom, should she give her report? She shifted her tote bag to the other hand and waited for a break in the traffic on busy East-West Highway. The police-woman who usually directed the traffic there had left and she would have to make it across on her own.

If it had been only her mother, or her mother and her real father. The traffic from the left slowed down and she ran across to the center island. I could be like Mary, she thought, and wait till someone asks for it. Now was her moment. The cars from the right were coming quickly. But there was time.

"Made it!" she said to herself when she reached the other side. She was about to start down the tarmac path that ran between the houses to her own street when she saw a figure ahead of her walking slowly and looking back occasionally. There was something famil-iar about the person—the way her hair was cut, the way her hips swung when she walked.

"Warning! Danger!" Julie said to herself. It looked very much like Rosalie, who lived down at the other end of Raymond Street and usually walked home with Cynthia, who lived at Julie's end, but on further. "Warning! Danger!" Instead of starting down the path, Julie turned right, down East-West Highway, purposefully, as though that was where she'd been intending to go all the time, in the opposite direction from where Rosalie lived.

She was probably waiting to ask me, Julie thought. She seemed the type. You could always hear her laughing louder than all the other girls in a group at the other end of the hall, the type who would ask a new girl, "How'd you do on your report? How'd you do in math?"

Julie walked faster. She had the unreasoning suspicion that Rosalie might follow her, that she might announce to the whole school that Julia M. Howard . . . (or was she Taylor? That was Stephen's last name. Her mom said she could choose which last name she wanted. It wasn't much of a choice. Only a name. She preferred her real father's, of course. Except that when her mom had a different last name, everyone would know that . . .) that Julia M. Howard had gotten a C-minus in math. Julie walked faster and faster. She turned left toward her own street. But when she was about to turn left again onto her street, she thought she saw Rosalie in the shadowy distance walking toward her. She might be coming to see Cynthia, Julie thought, and turned right. She felt somewhat ridiculous, almost running through the cold and the dark away from home, instead of toward it. What was she running from? From humiliation at school. From disgrace at home. In the cold and the dark all sorts of evil consequences from the C-minus in math seemed possible.

The street curved in a funny way so she thought she'd better turn left again in the direction of her house, and then she turned left a third time, which should have brought her home. But that street went off at a strange angle. At the next crossing, she wasn't sure whether to turn left or right, or should she go straight? Or should she try to go back the way she had come? She looked at the street sign. MORRIS STREET. She'd never heard of it, which wasn't surprising, since she was new to the area. Even though she'd only moved from the Virginia side of the District of Columbia to the Maryland side, the streets were unfamiliar except for a few main roads like Piney Branch and East-West Highway.

"Now what a fix I've got into," she said to herself. She felt tired and cold and the tote bag with her books seemed too heavy to carry any further. And it was really dark now. The streetlights were on and lights were on in many of the houses. "I guess I'm lost," she said to herself and it seemed like a complete statement of the way she felt.

"What should I do?" She summarized her alternatives. Keep walking. Go to a house and ask directions. Or ask someone she saw on the street, if she saw anyone. The last two alternatives meant speaking to strangers, and Julie, growing up in a large apartment complex where strangers could be very strange, had been admonished time and again never to speak to them. On the other hand, to walk further in what might prove to be the wrong direction when her arms hurt from carrying her books and her nose was running from the cold, so that she had to keep sniffing because she didn't have any tissues . . . . Julie looked up and down the street. Silence. No cars. Nobody walking. Then what about houses? She looked speculatively at the house on the corner. The lights were on in the living room and in a bedroom upstairs. Someone was changing into warm slippers and an old sweater before going down to sit in front of the fire. She was certain the rosy light in the living room was cast by wavering flames. Surely, people in such a house wouldn't be waiting to gobble up lost girls. Yet she hesitated. There was no light on at the front door. The house seemed closed away from her—warm and comfortable, while she was on the outside hungrily looking in. It was the way her own home had been for the past month since her mom and Stephen had gotten married. She was just a nuisance to them, when they really wanted to be alone together. And furthermore, some time she would have to tell them she'd gotten a C-minus in math. Or would she? She wouldn't be telling them anything unless she managed to find her way home.

At last some motion. A car appeared in the street halfway down the block and pulled into a driveway. She'd try to reach the person in the car. Julie started to run toward it, holding her tote bag in both arms. If she could only get to them and ask directions before they went into the house. "Hey," she wanted to call, "hey, can you tell me?" But she didn't have any breath left. The car door banged and the front door of the house banged before she could get there. Too late. "But I'll go and ring the bell and ask anyhow." While she waited a minute to catch her breath, she saw the lights of a bicycle crossing the street toward her—the red and orange reflectors and the spotlight on the handlebars.

"Wow," said the boy who was riding it, screeching

to a stop in front of her. "I'm late today." He grinned at her as though he knew her. "What are you doing over here?" he asked.

"How'd you know?" said Julie and she meant, How'd you know who I am? How'd you know I was lost?

"I know you," he said. "You just moved in across the street." From among the bare branches of the trees, the streetlight shone down on them, casting a halo around the boy's head. An archangel on a bicycle sent to rescue her. Julie thought of him as a special, miraculous being, not simply a boy. She didn't talk to boys if she could help it. She preferred having safely remote crushes on them. But this person had been sent to tell her how to find her way home.

"I don't know my way around too well yet," she said. Actually, she hated to admit she was lost.

"I can tell you how to get back," the boy said.

"Thank you," said Julie.

"Or I can show you, if you want to help me deliver my newspapers."

"Oh, no," said Julie, "I couldn't . . . ."

"I was only kidding," he said. "It's not hard. Go straight down this street to Piney Branch and left on Piney Branch and then—"

"Oh, sure," said Julie. "I should have guessed." It was that simple. Left from Piney Branch onto Raymond. Then up her driveway. She'd better hurry. Her mother might start to worry.

"Thanks," she said to the boy. Too bad he wasn't a girl, if he lived across the street from her. Too bad he wasn't Wendy.

When I get home, she decided as she walked along

Piney Branch and turned left onto Raymond, shifting her tote bag from hand to hand every thirty seconds, if Mom is alone, I'll get it over with. And it seemed as though the misery of the afternoon could be wiped out in the catharsis of telling her mother all about it. She looked down the street toward her house. Lights shone out from the hall and kitchen windows and the back-porch light was on. As she got closer, she saw that there were two cars in the driveway. Then Mom wouldn't be alone. Unless Stephen was upstairs changing and Mom was in the kitchen. She closed the back-porch door quietly and put her tote bag down on the chair. Before opening the door, she looked in through the window. Only her mom was there, washing dishes. Her own dear mom. She was about to burst in when Stephen entered the kitchen. Julie could see that he had changed from his business suit to his old trousers and plaid shirt. Even in his casual clothes he looked straight and formal. Not at all like her dad, whose clothes were always comfortably wrinkled and who always needed a haircut. Stephen went over to her mom, put his hands on her shoulders, and kissed her on the cheek. Then he noticed Julie's face at the window.

"Julie!" He came toward her, smiling. Julie picked up the tote bag and opened the door. The bag seemed ever so heavy with the brown envelope at the bottom. And now she'd have to wait until later to tell her mother about the C-minus. If she told her at all.

Where to Bury the Body?

Throughout dinner Julie kept thinking of the dead body buried in her room at the bottom of her tote bag. Was that a safe place to leave it? Would it be discovered? Through no fault of her own, she was being forced into the life of a criminal.

"Another hamburger?" her mother asked.

"Sure," said Julie. Crime must give one an appetite. At least skulking around back streets in Silver Spring and walking three times as far to get home in the cold with a cumbersome bag of books made one very hungry.

"More potato, too, please," Julie said.

"My, what an appetite!" Stephen exclaimed.

He's probably thinking I eat too much and I'm too expensive to have around, guessed Julie. Since her mother had married Stephen, nasty suspicions kept appearing in her brain unexpectedly, the way roaches would suddenly appear at night on the kitchen floor of their old apartment.

"How was school today?" asked Stephen. It was his usual way of starting a conversation with her.

"Fine," said Julie. It was so different with Stephen there and a tablecloth and candlelight, and all she said was "fine." Whereas, if it had been her mother alone asking her, she would have said, "Oh, Mom, the worst

thing happened today!" Well, why not? Why not say
that right now? Why not—?

"Have you had any tests?" Stephen asked. He was
getting close, very close to where the body was hidden.

"A few in math," said Julie, "but he never puts a
grade on them." It would be natural enough to say,
"And that's why I was so surprised today when . . . ."

But Stephen wouldn't understand. Her Mom
would, but Stephen didn't know her well enough.
He'd think she was dumb and didn't work and that
she was going to be a lot of trouble—a problem
child.

"I'm sure it's hard," her mother said. "Especially
with math, when it's all different from what you've had
before."

Oh, Mom, if only you knew, Julie thought.

There was a silence while everyone ate. I'd better
change the subject, she thought, away from school.

"I suppose it's too early for reports," Stephen said,
helping himself to more mashed potatoes.

Wow! He was right on top of the body. How could
she keep him from finding it? This time Mom inter-
vened.

"It doesn't matter anyhow," she said. "If they do
give grades after such a short period, it won't mean
anything." And she was a teacher, so she should know.
She looked at Julie reassuringly. Had she guessed?
Had Mrs. Barker called her? She'd heard of guidance
counselors doing sneaky things like that.

"I hope it's not too hard for you, dear. The change."
Her mother looked uncertain, as though she wasn't
sure but suspected difficulty.

Without answering her, Julie asked, "Shall I get dessert?" The change *was* too hard, and when she got her mother alone later, she'd tell her.

"Why, yes, dear. It's applesauce—in the refrigerator," her mother said.

Julie didn't realize how full the bowl was and took it out so quickly that some of the applesauce slopped onto the floor.

"Darn," she said out loud. Probably because I'm nervous, she thought.

"Can I help?" her mother called.

"No," said Julie. "I'll be right there." She got paper towels and started to wipe up the cold applesauce. I'm helpless, she thought. All I can do is mop up afterward. After my parents' divorce. After moving to a new school. I never get to make anything happen. It all happens to me.

She threw a mass of towels slimy with applesauce into the trash. If I didn't go back to the table, she thought, they wouldn't be able to ask me any more questions about school. But then they'd know something was wrong, so she went.

Her mom and Stephen weren't saying anything. "Think it'll snow?" Julie asked as she put the applesauce in front of her mother and returned to the kitchen for some bowls. The weather should be safe to talk about.

"It's supposed to," said Stephen. "According to Gordon Barnes on WTOP."

"Then it probably won't." Her mother laughed.

But it will, Julie decided. A special saving snow for me. A reprieve of one day or maybe more before she had to talk with Mrs. Barker about being tutored, before the kids at school were telling each other how dumb Julia M. Howard was.

"I already have snow tires on my car. What about yours?" Stephen asked her mother. Julie licked the applesauce off her spoon. Snow tires, and dinner was almost over, and they were safely diverted from the discussion of Julie and school. Snow tires could go on for a long time. She could remember Mom and Dad arguing about when to put them on. Mom always worried and Dad always said there was no hurry.

"They're on," said her mother, "but would you mind checking them? The treads may be—"

"May I be excused?" said Julie. She wanted to get back to the dead body and find a better hiding place for it.

"I started some mathematical analysis today that I'd really like to finish tomorrow," she heard Stephen saying as she carried her milk glass and applesauce dish out to the kitchen. Math, Stephen! Of course, Stephen knew all about math. Why not? Except that she didn't want to tell Stephen about the C-minus. She'd only explain that she needed help, which was true. Why not? Maybe she could arrange things so she didn't have to be tutored at school after all. Stepfathers might have some advantages.

When Julie was safely in her room with the door closed, she reached down into her tote bag under her books and got out her report. Where should she hide it? Under her mattress? Or why not on her desk under the pile of *True Romance* magazines—casually, as though it was something she'd gotten in the mail?

Except it didn't belong there with the happy end-

ings. That's what she read the *True Romance* stories for
—the real-life happy endings. "And then she knew
that he would never leave her side, that each year
together would be more beautiful than the one before." After all that had gone wrong in her life—parents divorced, a stepfather, and now the bad news in
the brown envelope—wasn't it time for a happy end-
ing?

She held the report out at arm's length and looked
at it. It didn't seem as repulsive as it had at school. It
seemed more like an innocent brown envelope and
less like a horrifying monster.

Julie went back, sat on her bed, took the pale green
memo sheets out of the envelope, and read each one
through. She read the math twice and the French three
times. It helped to confront it—to know the size and
shape of her problem.

"I've done my best," she said to herself. All along,
from the very beginning, when Mom and Dad sepa-
rated two years ago, and then a year later got divorced,
she'd done her best. That's what her grandmother had
told her to do when she and Dad had visited her in
Boston right after the separation. That was the last
time she'd seen her—Christmastime. Her grandmother was sitting to one side of the fire and she was
standing in front looking at the flames, trying to forget
that her mother wasn't there. Dad was out getting
more wood.

"Come over here by me, dear," Grandmother said.
As Julie sat on the arm of her chair and Grandmother
took hold of her hand, she said, "It'll be hard, dear,
but you have to help all you can."

Julie had leaned against her grandmother and said in a whisper, "Maybe I didn't help enough and that's why. . . ."

"No, you dear," Grandmother said. "You have nothing to do with it." Then her father came back with a big log, which he put right on the fire, where it sparkled and danced, looking more cheerful than any of them felt. That was all she and her grandmother ever said about the divorce.

Well, she might not have been responsible for her parents' divorce, but Julie knew it was her fault that her mother had married Stephen. If she had taken Stephen seriously, it might not have happened. But she had assumed that he wasn't important. When Mom got divorced, she'd said she was through getting involved with men. And Julie believed her. So she didn't pay much attention when Mom started going out with Stephen last winter just before the divorce was granted. He was someone to take Mom to nice restaurants for dinner, which Julie knew she enjoyed, and to plays at the Kennedy Center. That's the way she looked at it.

When Stephen was around the apartment for a meal now and then, if he seemed awkward about talking with her, she didn't make an effort to help him.

"How's school?" Stephen would usually start.

"Okay," Julie would say. Then, "May I be excused?" And she'd leave to watch TV or do her homework. But in September something happened.

Julie had gone to spend the night at Wendy's apartment down the hall. During dinner she hadn't felt very hungry, and when they were watching *The Yellow Sub-*

marine on TV she became increasingly certain that she had a fever. The movie seemed even weirder than it really was, the colors brighter and blurred together, the music jarring and painful.

After putting her palm against Julie's forehead, Wendy's mom said there was no doubt that she had a fever. Julie remembered it so clearly; Wendy's mother said, "You'd probably be more comfortable in your own bed." Julie agreed. She felt awful. She wanted to get back to her mother as quickly as possible.

If she hadn't felt so dizzy, she wouldn't have been willing to walk down the hall to her own apartment in her bathrobe. Fortunately, since it was late, eleven o'clock, there was no one around. Wendy's mother walked down with her.

"Can you manage?" she asked as Julie unlocked the apartment door.

"Sure," said Julie. Barely, she thought. But the best help, her mother, was now near at hand.

"Mom!" Julie called as she closed the door behind her. The living room was dark. Mom must have gone to bed. "Mom," she called again, weakly. She couldn't collapse yet, not until she'd gotten to her. She stumbled across the living room into the little hall. There was no light shining under the bedroom door. Julie opened it quietly and then, because she couldn't stand any longer, knelt down beside her mother's sleeping form.

"I'm sick, Mom," she said. She felt as though she might spit up. A face turned toward her and she heard Stephen's voice.

"Marjorie!" he said.

"Where is she?" asked Julie, thinking her mother was somewhere else. But then Mom sat up on the other side of Stephen.

And she was so glad to see her mother that she didn't mind about Stephen. Not until she thought about it later. When she wasn't feverish any longer, only drained and rubbery feeling, she experienced fully the shock of finding Stephen in her mother's bed and then finding her mother there with him.

She thought back over what she had seen. They were asleep when she came in. She hadn't interrupted anything. But before her unexpected arrival? Her mind stopped at that point, resisting further conclusions. I never want to see Stephen again, ever, ever, Julie thought.

Mom didn't apologize or explain. Not directly. But when Julie was better, she came and sat at the foot of her bed and said, "I wanted to talk to you, dear." She patted Julie's foot. Julie pulled it away from her. "This may be a surprise. Or you may have already guessed . . ."

I haven't, thought Julie to herself. And she didn't want to.

"I decided to wait until you were better to tell you that"—her mother finished quickly—"Stephen and I *are* planning to get married." As though that made everything all right. And Julie was convinced that by blundering into her mother's room that night, she had been the unwitting cause of their marriage. Mom felt she had to make it all legal and proper for Julie's sake.

Julie looked down at the green sheets of her report, thinking of the consequences: the move from Virginia, the new school, the C-minus in math, and looming over everything else the permanence of Stephen's presence in their lives, especially (and she saw again the dark image of Stephen's face lifted from the pillow) in her mother's bed.

"No, I don't know where it is." She could hear Mom calling downstairs to Stephen. "I'll ask Julie."

Caught, holding the incriminating evidence! There was no time to put the green sheets back in the envelope. Quickly, put it all under the magazines! Julie hopped across the room. One foot was asleep. Her mother was knocking on the door and calling, "Julie!"

"What is it, Mom?" In her haste, Julie almost upset her precious rabbit fern in the blue pot, which she had brought with her from Virginia.

"Have you seen Stephen's *Audubon* magazine? Can I come in a moment?"

"What's it look like?" said Julie, trying to sound casual rather than breathless. Her mother opened the door.

"Can I come in?"

"Sure," said Julie, moving away from the desk.

"I guess it has a bird on the front."

"An osprey," said Stephen, who had come up behind her mother.

"No, I haven't seen anything like that," said Julie. Stephen and his birds! He was nuts about birds, dragging her mom out on bird walks and keeping lists of birds he had seen. Lifetime lists! And hanging up bird feeders and suet sticks.

"What about over there?" Stephen pointed to the pile of magazines on her desk.

"They're all mine," said Julie. She didn't want to say
that they were *True Romance*.

"Mind if I check?" Stephen asked.

"That's okay, I'll look. But I'm sure."

"Thanks, dear," said her mother.

"Sorry to bother you," said Stephen. With Mom and
Stephen both watching, Julie looked through the
magazines, careful not to lift the bottom one.

"I don't understand," said Stephen. "I always put it
in my briefcase."

"It's not here," said Julie.

"How about the car?" her mother suggested.

"I don't think so," said Stephen, "but I'll look."

While Stephen left to look in the car, her mom
waited at the door. Then she came over and sat down
on the bed. Julie was still standing by the desk.

"Mind if we talk?" Mom asked.

"No," said Julie and swallowed. This was the moment she had been waiting for. She and her mother
were alone together. But it was very hard to get
started. Especially after her evasiveness at dinner, especially when it would be obvious that she had tried
to hide her report under the *True Romance* magazines.
Or could she pull it out as though she had that moment thought of it and say, "Oh, Mom, I meant to give
this to you when I got home." She couldn't. It wasn't
true, and she couldn't pretend it was.

"Julie,"—her mother was sounding very firm—"I
know something's wrong and I want you to tell me
what it is." That was her mom. She looked so soft and
pretty, tonight especially with her fuzzy slippers and
her lavender velour sweat shirt, as though you could

get her to do anything you wanted. But underneath she could be as hard to move as the Washington Monument. Julie guessed that was what Dad had been surprised to discover after they were married.

"Come on, sweetie,"—Mom patted the bed beside her—"sit down here and tell me about it."

Acting was easier than talking. Julie pulled the green papers out from under the pile of magazines and handed them to her. The math was on top, but it was too late to shift it.

"It's my report," she explained.

"Oh," said Mom, taking the papers from Julie with just the slightest look of "Oh-ho, so I was right" on her face.

Julie stood in front of her mother as she read, and then, since she felt awkward, sat down on the bed next to her. Having never before gotten a bad grade, she didn't know how Mom would react. Well, she couldn't blame Julie. She'd have to blame herself first for making Julie change schools in the middle of the year.

"Mom, don't tell Stephen," Julie said.

"About what?" said her mother. But of course she knew. She was trying to make it seem unimportant.

"You know, Mom. About the math," Julie said.

"I know, Julie. It's an unpleasant experience, but it doesn't mean a thing," her mother said. "It's nothing to be ashamed of. Math teachers are that way. It's all numerical with them. They don't allow for special circumstances. Look at how wonderful your other grades are."

"It's only that now I have to be tutored or get help somehow and I thought maybe—"

"Marjorie!" Stephen was calling from the foot of the stairs.

"Did you find it?" her mother called back.

"Do you know what I found?" Stephen shouted. He sounded too agitated to listen to her.

"I hope you found the *Audubon* magazine!" her mom called back again.

"Come here, I'll show you. Unless you don't like to see sickening things."

"I don't," she answered. "Neither does Julie." Julie knew that was her mother's way of making sure Stephen remembered to include her. "Shall we finish our talk later?" her mother asked Julie. She was already standing.

"Sure," said Julie. That's the way it was. Now Stephen needed attention.

By the time they got downstairs, Stephen was out on the back porch. He was holding something in a piece of newspaper.

"Do we have a shoe box to put it in," he asked, "until I can bury it?"

Julie looked cautiously at the brown thing that was lying on the newspaper. It was a dead bird. The horrible part was that its neck seemed to be broken and one wing almost twisted off.

"Oh, Stephen," said Mom.

"What kind is it?" said Julie. Mutilated as it was, the brown feathers still suggested warmth and life.

"A white-throated sparrow," said Stephen, tenderly cupping his hands around the small body, "a ground feeder."

"Poor little thing," Mom said. "Was it a squirrel or . . . ?"

"Probably a cat," said Stephen. "There's a yellow one I keep chasing."

"Where'd you find it?" Julie asked. She was impressed with how much Stephen, who had always seemed so severe and unemotional, cared about a dead bird—a common sparrow. Not one of the rare birds that he could add to his list.

"By your mother's car," he said, "when I turned the light on to look at the tires."

While Stephen waited, mourning the bird, Mom went off to get a box. No one was thinking about Julie and her report card, except Julie.

What will I tell Mrs. Barker? she wondered as she watched Stephen cradle the bird in his hands.

"Are you going to bury it?" Julie asked.

"Not right away," Stephen said. "The ground's frozen and, oh yes, I forgot. You'll be glad to hear, Julie. It's starting to snow."

"Gordon Barnes was right for once," said Mom, handing a small, rectangular soap box to Stephen. "Will this do?"

Stephen put the dead sparrow into the soap box with all the care and concentration of a little boy packing away a treasure.

"Now what?" said Mom.

"I thought we'd keep it in the freezer," said Stephen, "till the ground thaws and I can bury it."

"The freezer! You're crazy," said Mom.

"You don't have to look at it," Stephen urged. "It won't be long. The weather's always changing here."

Julie waited for them to have an argument, but Mom said, "I'll tape it closed," and took the box from Stephen.

Romance, thought Julie. People'll do anything when they're in love with each other.

"Does someone know where the tape is?" her mother called from the kitchen.

"In the drawer by the sink." Stephen went in to help her look.

Eventually, Mom would remember about Julie and math. Then Julie could ask about having Stephen help her. Without telling him of course about . . . . But why was it she always had to wait for the grown-ups in her life to solve their problems first? Even small problems, like Stephen and his dead bird.

She opened the porch door and looked out. Nothing visible on the ground. Was Stephen mistaken? She looked over toward the light on the side of the garage. No, it was coming down for sure. A myriad of tiny, busy flakes of snow swirled in front of the light. It was the kind of snow that kept on going. Soon the ground would be covered. And tomorrow . . . .

As Julie went back through the kitchen, Mom said, "Shall we finish our talk?" Julie looked at Stephen, he was fitting the soap box with the bird in it into the freezer. He still seemed upset. Maybe tomorrow would be a better time to ask him to help her with math.

"How about tomorrow?" Julie suggested.

"All right," said Mom. "If it snows we'll have all day."

Julie went on up to her room. The pale green sheets of paper were lying on the bed where Mom had left them. She put them back into the envelope.

Too bad I can't leave this in the freezer, she thought, and bury it when it thaws.

Snow Day

"Would you like to do a little shoveling?" Stephen asked the next morning in a way that was more like a command.

"If you'll help me with math," Julie was tempted to say, but she didn't think she should until she'd discussed it with her mother. She felt warm and full of bacon and eggs and cocoa. Ready to do anything for anyone.

"Get away, go home!" Stephen started knocking on the kitchen window. Then he rushed out the back door. "Go home, shoo!" Julie could hear his shouting echo through the frosty morning air.

"He went out in his slippers!" Julie looked toward her mother for an explanation.

"It's the yellow cat, I expect," her mother said, calmly sipping her coffee. Julie went over to the window. She could see Stephen standing under the bird feeder waving his arms and a mustard-colored cat sprinting over the side fence. He turned and ran back to the house. Julie could hear him on the back porch stamping off the snow.

"Now, if Julie will shovel"—he was back inside, leaning against the counter, warming his hands around a coffee cup—"I'll walk over to the plaza for more sunflower seed."

"I'm sorry, I had it on my shopping list, but I

couldn't find it," her mother said. "I hate to have you walk so far, though I suppose it's easier than brushing off the car."

Julie remembered looking out the window after her alarm went off and seeing the snow deep on the street and on the cars parked along it. She had gone back to sleep confident that everything would be closed—all the schools, all the federal offices in the enormous white buildings. And it was still coming down. Now, while her mother and Stephen talked, she watched each fascinating snowflake fall.

"It's a challenge," Stephen said. "Where's your pioneer spirit? And if Julie . . . ."

Julie blinked. She was being mesmerized by the snow. "I'm on my way," she said. She left to get her jacket and the mittens and scarf her Boston grandmother had knitted for her. Shoveling snow would be fun. It was something she hadn't gotten to do in Virginia.

But there were always plenty of kids in Virginia, she remembered as she stood outside the back door. The white world seemed unnaturally quiet and empty. No voices calling, no parking lot snowball fights. No Wendy to build a snowman with, hurrying to finish before the lot was plowed.

Only one boy across the street, she thought, as she clomped to the garage for the snow shovel. An older boy, she thought, as she took giant steps down the driveway. She looked along the street. Someone was walking toward her using the tracks made by the few cars that had ventured out, a girl with a blue pom-pom hat and long, blond hair. It was Cynthia. A possible friend. Maybe they could do something together—have lunch, listen to records. Maybe, if she was going to Rosalie's, all three of them could . . . .

"Hi," she called out to Cynthia. "Great, isn't it?"

"Hi, honey. Sure is. Except it's so difficult to walk. You-all going to do some shoveling?"

"A little," said Julie.

"My daddy's home shoveling our path," said Cynthia.

"My . . . ." Julie never knew what to call Stephen in public. "I said I'd do ours. But it won't take long." Julie wanted Cynthia to know that she'd have time to do something afterward.

"Cold, isn't it?" said Cynthia. "I never can seem to get used to the winter. I guess I'd better start moving before I freeze to death."

"Guess so," said Julie.

"See you tomorrow." Cynthia waved. "Or the next day. If we're lucky."

"Bye," said Julie. She felt much lonelier than she had before. She pushed the snow shovel slowly along the path and lifted a pile of snow off to the side. But Cynthia and Rosalie together might have asked her about her report. That was a good reason to stay away from them until the excitement over report cards had melted the way the snow would melt.

Shoveling made Julie's arms ache. And her back was starting to hurt from bending over for so long. She stood upright and leaned on the shovel to rest.

The wind seemed calmer and the snow less driving. In the silence, there was an air of mystery. The red brick houses veiled with snow looked strangely sub-

dued. But the house that really made her shiver was
the house across the street and to the left.

Julie peered at it through the snow. It was like someone's dream, or nightmare. The crazy pattern of tur-
rets and gables suggested that there were all sorts of
unexpected nooks and crannies inside. It was painted
gray, with each eccentric projection topped by a white
shroud of snow. In the back, the black tops of three
dark evergreens projected above the roofs like evil
wizards with white pointed caps.

"Think it's haunted?" a voice asked behind her.
Julie jumped and turned. The boy from across the
street stood there with a snow shovel in his hand. He
had on a green cap with a visor and flaps over his ears.
"Think it has ghosts inside?"

Julie stared at him. Was he making fun of her?
Treating her like a little girl? Behind his big, round
glasses with metal rims, his brown eyes seemed
friendly, companionable. Julie felt nervous. Boys
made her uncomfortable. They were always busy
wrestling and throwing snowballs. She chose to ideal-
ize them from a distance, because when she got near
them, they never stayed quiet long enough to talk to.
But this one was still standing there, leaning on his
snow shovel, waiting for her to answer.

"I don't know," said Julie. "Since I just moved
here." She looked back at the house. Through the mist
of snow, now falling more sparsely, it seemed separate, aloof, as though it belonged to another world.

"It was here first," the boy said, "before any of the
other houses."

"Those trees look old," Julie said. She pointed to
the tall, dark pine trees behind the house.

"And the people who lived in it owned all this." He gestured up and down the street.

"Who lives there now?" Julie asked. It was so easy to talk with this boy who stood still and kept smiling at her.

"An old, old woman," he said. "A witch," he hissed, bending close to her. Julie put her hand over her ear and laughed.

"I'm Cal," he said, straightening up. "Who are you?"

"Cal?" Julie wanted to be sure she had it right.

"Short for California," he said, with a slight bow. Julie had never talked to such a funny, agreeable boy.

"And you are," he insisted.

"Julie."

"Short for?" he asked.

"Nothing interesting," Julie said. "Just Julia."

"You've got it wrong," Cal said. "It's short for Jewel."

Was he making fun of her? Julie couldn't decide.

"I'll race you, Jewel." Cal turned to leave.

"Race me, where?" Julie asked. Boys were always doing vigorous, athletic things that she wasn't any good at.

"Clearing paths. I'll clear our path before you finish yours." This was a race Julie thought she could manage. But she had to be fair.

"I have a head start," she pointed out.

"But I," said Cal, "am older and wiser. And I'll beat you anyhow!" He ran in big steps back across the street. "Ready, set, go!" he shouted. They both started shoveling. Once, very quickly, Julie looked up and saw a little boy in a bright blue snowsuit come out of the house. She didn't stop to watch, but kept on shoveling.

"Whatcha doing, Cal?" she heard him call out.

"Don't bother me, kid, I'm racing."

Then after a minute she heard his voice next to Cal saying, "Can I help?"

"Be a good little brother and go help Jewel over there. She needs it."

"Jewel who?" said the little boy.

"No, I don't," said Julie. "I'm almost finished."

"Well, I *am* finished," said Cal.

"I don't believe it." Julie stopped and stood up to look. The sidewalk in front of Cal's house was clear from driveway to driveway. He had even done the steps. Cal was coming toward her.

"I'll help you, and then you can help me."

"How?" said Julie. "If you're all finished."

"The haunted house," said Cal. "My mom told me to do it, because ghosts can't shovel snow."

"You mean old ladies can't shovel snow," said Cal's little brother, who had come up right behind him.

"He means witches can't shovel snow," said Julie.

"That's right," Cal agreed. "They don't need to." He and Julie shoveled as they talked.

"They just ride up above the snow on their broomsticks," said Cal's little brother. "But I know she's not a witch. I asked Mom, and she said she was only old Mrs. Mitchell. That's all. And she was born like anyone else. She was a little baby once with a pointy, sharp nose and pointy, sharp teeth."

"And gray hair in a little knot on the top of her head? Be careful, child. If she hears you disbelieving in her, she might turn you into a snowman."

"Does she really look that awful?" asked Julie.

"And when it got warm, you would melt away into nothing," Cal persisted. "Quickly, you'd better go hide in the house where she can't catch you."

"Cal, you're teasing," his little brother said. But his eyes looked big, as though he was frightened.

"That's it for your house," said Cal lifting the shovel to his shoulder. "Come on, Jewel." He gave a jerk to the end of her red scarf, pulling it loose so it hung down her back.

"What's your little brother's name?" asked Julie as they crossed the street.

"Captain Crunch. Crunch, for short," said Cal.

"You don't expect me to believe you!" said Julie.

"Ask him. Go ahead. He'll tell you." Cal turned to start shoveling.

Julie looked down toward Cal's house and saw his little brother disappearing around the side.

"I will," said Julie, "when he comes back. Where shall I shovel?"

"You go the other way," Cal said, "and we'll both do the steps."

Julie's hands felt cold, so she squeezed them into fists inside her mittens to warm them. She held her shovel in the crook of her arm while she stood warming her hands and looking toward the old house. If houses were ever haunted, this one certainly was. At least there was something secret about it. All the shades were pulled. There was no window in the front door. The house was closed in upon itself—today especially, with a magic cloak of white snow thrown over it and dark, sentinel trees hovering behind it.

"What's all that around the door?" Julie asked when

she and Cal were shoveling the front path together.

"Spells," said Cal. "Can't you feel their power?"

"I guess you know I don't believe anything you say," Julie answered.

"You'll be sorry," said Cal, "I've tried to protect you."

"I'm going to read them myself," said Julie, starting up the steps to the porch.

"Look out!" called Cal in such a warning voice that Julie turned to look behind her. She felt foolish when she saw the grin on Cal's face. She wasn't sure whether he wanted to be friendly with her or whether he wanted to make fun of her. If Cal was an example of what boys were like, they were certainly hard to figure out.

"Don't worry, Jewel. I'll rescue you," he called as she crossed the old wooden porch to the front door. The door looked as though it had never been opened and never would be. But someone had come out to pin up all the cards around it. Someone who had started to do it a long time ago.

There were cards that were wrinkled and dirty and spotted from rain being blown in on them. Then there were cards that were fresh and white. Some had flowers on them. One was in the shape of a cross. Julie leaned her snow shovel against the gray siding and took off her mittens to blow on her hands while she read.

> Seek, and ye shall find;
> Knock, and it shall be opened unto you.
> *Matthew 7:6*

She looked toward the front door. Of course it didn't mean that door and that house. She knew it was from the Bible. She knew it was talking about God. Still, for one minute, she had an uncomfortable feeling that God was the secret of the house, that God was there. God in the form of an old woman with a pointy nose and pointy teeth. God wasn't magic, she told herself. And God wasn't ugly.

On the other side of the door, she saw a picture of a handsome, strong, bearded young man carefully holding a baby lamb in his arms as though not to wake it. Underneath it said:

Like a Shepherd He Careth for Thee.

The picture was beautiful. Almost too beautiful. The sky was too blue and the grass was too green. Yet Julie felt a kinship with the young man who was carrying the lamb so carefully.

"You've stopped moving," Cal called out. "You're turning to ice. Can you feel it?" he called. " 'It starts at your toes and the tips of your nose and slowly it goes . . . .' "

How strange they were, these feelings of religion and magic mixed up together. Julie looked around the door again and then at the door itself. What if it should open? Suddenly, she felt scared. And standing on the other side would be . . . .

"Oooooohhhh! Help!" Julie called out. Something was tugging at her scarf, pulling, pulling. Would it pull her inside? "Ooooohhhh!" she screamed again. And then she thought, of course, it's only Cal.

"You!" she said, turning around. The tugging stopped. There was no one there. Cal was still standing down on the path. He was laughing.

Julie's eyes widened with fear and excitement. The tugging started again. Quickly, Julie turned back toward the door and looked down. Then she knew why Cal was laughing. A gray-striped tabby cat with white paws was pulling on the end of her red scarf.

"Oh," said Julie. "Oh." She leaned over toward the cat so it wouldn't pull so hard and tried to stroke it.

"Who are you?" she said. "And what do you think you're doing?" Keeping the end of the scarf in its mouth, the cat started to walk around Julie so that she and the cat were getting twisted up in it. "You silly thing," she said, laughing. "Let go!" She tried to reach the cat. "Cal, help!"

Cal put down his shovel and came up on the porch. He picked up the cat, and as he did so it let go of the scarf. The cat settled down in his arms as though that was where it most wanted to be. Cal took off a glove so that he could stroke it. He started up by its ears and smoothed its fur down to its tail.

"Poor Cal," Julie said, "your hand's all red with cold."

"Can't feel a thing," said Cal. "Must be frostbite." It was a nice hand—big, but gentle.

"You look like the picture," said Julie. And she pointed to the picture of the shepherd holding the baby lamb.

"I'd be in trouble if I let my hair grow that long," said Cal. "Here, it's your turn to hold it." He started to hand the cat to Julie.

"I don't know anything about cats," said Julie, hesitating. In that moment the cat jumped down from Cal's arms and started along the freshly shoveled path.

"Oh," said Julie. She was disappointed, but a little bit relieved. Cats might bite or scratch. A rabbit fern was much safer.

"I bet you've named it Dracula," she said.

"Definitely. That's what I would call it, if it was mine," said Cal, sitting down on the top step.

"It isn't yours?" said Julie, sitting down next to him.

"Wish it were," said Cal. "Or a dog."

"Then why not?" Julie asked. "You don't live in an apartment."

"An allergic sibling," said Cal.

"Captain Crunch?"

Cal nodded. "To just about everything."

"So you don't have any choice?" asked Julie. It happened to other people, too. Being put in boxes you couldn't get out of.

"Between goldfish and a salamander."

"All I have is a rabbit fern," said Julie.

"Really?" Cal seemed interested. "That's unusual." He had both gloves off and was blowing on his hands.

"With furry roots that grow up above the ground."

"That's not a very active pet."

"But I brought it from Virginia."

"Where you lived before?"

"Yes."

"I see," Cal said. "That makes a difference." Julie felt that he understood what it meant to leave all your friends at school and your best friend at home.

"Pets that can move around are better," Cal said. "But you have to do more for them."

"I like that part," Julie said.

"You can't just water them." Cal tried to look very serious and knowing. Then he said suddenly, "Come on, Jewel. In another moment, we will have turned into ice sculpture. Let's find Captain Crunch and build a snowman." He grabbed the end of her red scarf and pulled it so that it came off all together. She ran after him to catch it and then remembered her snow shovel.

"Wait!" she called and ran back to the porch. As she took hold of the shovel, she paused to look at the door. Did anyone in there know what they'd done, that they'd shoveled the path? Did anyone care? For the first time, she saw a big sign over the door that said:

ARE YOU SAVED?

From what? Would someone open the door and ask her? She hurried to catch up with Cal.

"Does she ever come out?" Julie asked.

"On Groundhog Day," said Cal. Cal was teasing her again, but it didn't worry her. He seemed to like her. Didn't he want to build a snowman with her? If she ever did see Mrs. Mitchell, she hoped Cal was around so they could discuss her.

When they paused at the foot of Cal's driveway, Julie snatched her scarf back from Cal and wound it around her neck again. Cal's little brother came along the driveway from the back of the house.

"Wanta help me build a snowman?" he called out.

As Julie and Cal started to follow him, Julie saw someone walking toward them on the other side of the street, someone who was wearing a bright blue hat with a pom-pom on it. Cynthia must have finished her visit with Rosalie already. It must be lunchtime by now. Should she go home? Julie looked over at her house for an answer, but it wasn't giving one. No one seemed to be looking out for her. Seeing Cynthia also made her wonder whether she was too old to build snowmen. Well, Cal was even older than she was.

"Come on, Jewel," Cal called. "Captain Crunch and I are waiting for you. The snow will melt if we don't hurry." Julie waved to Cynthia, who was now almost across from them, and turned to follow Cal.

"I'm coming," she said. He'd already gone. For a moment she wondered if she should follow.

"Julie!" His little brother was back. "Cal won't start without you."

"I'm coming," Julie said again and ran after him.

There was a path cleared along the side of the driveway around to the back of the house. At the end of the path, after it turned the corner, Julie was surprised to find the cat.

"Why, hello," Julie said. The cat came toward her with its back arched and rubbed its side against her leg. When Julie stooped down to stroke it, the cat put both paws up on her knee and looked at her. It seemed to be explaining something.

"Where do you live?" said Julie. "You're such a friendly cat."

"It's a stray," said Cal's little brother.

"Some kid on the street told him he was moving to Chicago and leaving the cat behind," Cal explained.

"Leaving behind a nice, sociable cat like this!" said Julie. As she stood up, the cat squeezed between her legs and then went over and rubbed itself against Cal's little brother. He stood very still and straight with his arms down at his sides.

"Think it'll hurt, Cal?" he asked.

"Not in the fresh air." Cal had a handful of snow that he was working into a snowball.

"Wish we could keep it," said Cal's little brother.

"It'd be a nice pet," said Julie. "Better than a rabbit fern."

"Yeah," said Cal, starting to roll the snowball over and over on the snowy ground. The snow was moist enough to stick to the snowball on each turn. Cal didn't say anything to make his little brother feel bad about being allergic.

"I'd have a problem, too," said Julie. And she was about to say, "My stepfather's always chasing cats." But she still didn't want people to know that she had a stepfather. It made her seem like a failure, like someone who got C-minuses in math.

"What's your problem, Jewel?" asked Cal, turning his snowball, which was as big as a watermelon, over on its side because it was only plump in one direction and needed to fatten up the other way.

"Oh, it's nothing," said Julie. "Except . . ."—she had to think of something to say—"I want to know," she said to Cal's little brother, who was still standing stiffly even though the cat was walking back toward the driveway, "what your name is."

"Rumplestiltskin," said Cal, over his shoulder. He was kneeling in the snow now, pushing his burgeoning snowball with both hands.

"That's just in a book," said Cal's little brother. "That's not my name."

"Well, what is it?" said Julie. "Don't interrupt, Cal. Let him answer."

"Captain Crunch," said the little boy, jumping up and down. "Captain Crunch, that's what Cal calls me. And then"—he ran over toward Cal—"he calls me Crunch for short." He threw himself on top of Cal, who was still kneeling over his snowball, and they both collapsed on top of it. "Oh, Crunch!" said Cal. Then Cal got up on all fours and started crawling through the snow with Captain Crunch on his back. "Jingle Bells," he started singing.

"Jingle all the way," Julie joined in.

"Come on, Jewel," Cal called. "Be the one-horse open sleigh."

"What about the snowman?" Julie asked.

"Right," said Cal. "It's cold down here."

As he stood up, Captain Crunch slid to the ground. "Time we got to work. You do the middle, Jewel, Crunch, you do the head. And because I'm halfway through, I'll do the bottom, which has to be super-big."

"You think you're so great, Cal," said Captain Crunch, still lying in the snow and holding onto Cal's ankles. Cal took a few steps, dragging Captain Crunch along with him. Then Captain Crunch let go and stood up, brushing off his snowy front.

"Race you," said Cal.

"Not again," said Julie. "You're practically finished already anyhow."

"I've only gotten to the hard part. The hard-to-push part," said Cal.

Julie and Captain Crunch both launched their snowballs while Cal struggled and groaned over his enormous one.

"Where do you go to school?" Julie asked while they were working.

"Same as you," said Cal.

"You aren't just kidding again?"

"What do you mean?" said Cal. "I never kid anyone. Do I, Crunch?"

"I've never seen you," said Julie.

"That's 'cause I'm in the ninth grade." Cal's snowball and hers were on a collision path.

"So?" said Julie, turning hers to the right. The entire yard was becoming crisscrossed with paths made by rolling snowballs.

"Ninth graders are invisible," said Cal. "Now it's time to put your snowball on top of mine."

"You must be," said Julie, "anyhow."

"All the best ninth graders are," said Cal as he helped Julie to hoist her snowball up.

"Careful, don't let it fall apart. Here, Crunch, give us a hand. Over this way a little. We don't want a lopsided snowman."

Now that she knew Cal went to the same school, Julie wanted to ask him whether he'd ever had Mr. Hawkins for math.

"We've got a nice, plump snowman going here," Cal said.

"Here's the head," said Captain Crunch.

"Not yet!" Cal put out a detaining hand. "This gentleman must have a neck."

"A neck?" said Captain Crunch.

"So he can wear Jewel's scarf."

"But I want to wear it," said Julie.

"Won't you let him try it on"—Cal knelt down in the snow with his hands clasped—"for a minute? Won't you?"

"Only to see how he looks," said Julie. Cal was hard to resist. She really did want to ask him about Mr. Hawkins, but she was afraid that he might ask her a question she didn't want to answer. Still, as they were fitting the head onto the neck, she said, "Cal, did you ever have Mr. Hawkins for math?" and she knew her voice sounded shaky when she said it.

"That horror?" said Cal, and he looked at her. "No one ever survives his class, without being pulverized," he said. He smiled at her. "And learning a lot," he continued. And he didn't ask her the question. "That's a good name for our snowman," he said. "Mr. Hawkins. Cold as infinity."

When Mr. Hawkins was finished, looking very athletic with the red scarf, Julie decided that she really must go home for lunch. The prospect was a lonely one, but there was no way she could invite Cal to come back as she would have invited Wendy. She didn't know him well enough and he was a boy and he might not care about coming, since he had Captain Crunch. Whereas, she had no one even near her own age. Only Mom and Stephen. And they'd probably eaten already.

"I think I'd better go," said Julie, starting to unwind her red scarf."

"Just a minute," said Cal. "Where to?"

"Home for lunch," said Julie. She hoped Cal would suggest doing something in the afternoon.

"You won't wear your scarf while you eat, will you?"

"It would get all messy," objected Captain Crunch seriously.

"And leave Mr. Hawkins out here in danger of getting a chill?"

"No more than he deserves," said Julie. But she dropped the scarf. "I'll get it later," she said. That might be a way of seeing Cal, and then he might ask her to do something—go for a walk or sledding. She hadn't done that since her last trip to Boston.

"See you," said Julie as she left.

"See you," said Cal.

"Bye," said Captain Crunch.

As Julie walked slowly down the driveway, across the street, and up her own driveway, the uncertainty of the future drifted through the chilly air with the last few solitary snowflakes, latecomers in the storm.

Back to Mr. Hawkins

Julie thought she would eat lunch as quickly as possible and get back to working on Mr. Hawkins. She meant to hurry so as to be there before Cal and Captain Crunch left.

"Your dad wants you to call," her mother said as she came into the kitchen.

"I'll do it later," said Julie.

"Better call now," her mother insisted. "He said he's going out soon."

"Okay," said Julie. She ran upstairs to call because it made her feel strange to have Mom listen when she talked to Dad on the phone.

"Let's do something on Saturday," he said.

"Sure," agreed Julie. She wanted to see him. She'd only been with him once since Mom and Stephen were married. He'd come and taken her to a matinee and for ice cream afterward. But she didn't want to spend a lot of time making arrangements.

"How about the zoo?"

"Fine," said Julie. It wasn't really. It sounded cold. But she didn't want to discuss it.

"Do you mind coming by metro?" Dad had moved too. In Virginia, he had lived in an apartment building a few blocks away. It had been easy for Julie to run over and see him any time, or to take Wendy with her. Now he lived in the District on Connecticut Avenue.

"You can take the bus. Or your mom can drive you to the Takoma metro stop," her father said. "And I'll drive you home. You don't mind?" he said again.

In a way she did, because she'd never done it before. In another way, she was glad, because it made her more grown-up and independent if she could get places on the metro. There was no time to explain all of that.

"No, I don't," she said.

"That's my girl," he applauded. "Let me tell your mom. See you Saturday, monkey."

Julie ran back down to the kitchen. "Dad wants to talk to you," she said. "Any soup left?"

"Yes, I kept it hot," said Mom. Julie hoped it wasn't too hot as that would really slow her down. Her mother picked up the receiver and stepped out into the hall so Julie couldn't hear what she was saying.

She must feel the same way, thought Julie.

She didn't talk long. When she came back, Julie had just started her soup.

"Can we chat for a minute?" she asked.

If it's only a minute, Julie thought. "Okay," she said. The soup was too hot anyhow. "It's all right with me," she said, "about the metro."

"Yes," said her mother, "I want to talk about that too. But first I wanted to talk about your math."

"Oh, that," said Julie. Math would take more than a minute. And she didn't want to think about it now. She wanted to get back to the snow and Cal and Captain Crunch.

"Didn't your teacher say something about your needing help?"

"Yes," said Julie. The soup was starting to cool, so

she could spoon it up more rapidly. Soon she'd be able to drink it down. But now she was caught in a discussion with Mom about math.

"Did your teacher have any suggestions? Or your guidance counselor?"

"My guidance counselor said I should be tutored. And, Mom, I thought maybe Stephen could do it. I mean without telling him anything. Only that I need help because it's all new. He knows a lot about math."

"Well . . . ." Mom frowned.

"It would be cheaper," Julie urged.

"Well . . . ." Mom took a deep breath. "Let's think about it," she said.

"You mean later?" Julie stood up. She was ready to put her dishes in the dishwasher.

"No, let's do it now," her mother said, "while we have the time."

"But I don't—" Julie started to say. Then she sat down. Might as well get it over with. Maybe there'd be school tomorrow and then it would be good to have a plan ready for Mrs. Barker.

"It's a nice thought," her mother continued, "but I wonder whether Stephen could really . . . give you . . . the kind of help you need."

"He knows all about math, doesn't he?"

"Yes, but it's so different from what you're learning."

"So it should be easy for him. I remember Dad—" Julie stopped herself. She never felt comfortable talking about her dad, especially with her mother.

"Look, Mom." Julie stood up again. "I want to go back outside. Why don't I ask Stephen later and see what he thinks?" Julie said it rapidly, because she heard Stephen coming up from the basement. He must have been painting the new bookcase. Julie could smell the fumes.

"Why not ask him now, and get it settled?" her mother suggested.

"I'd rather—"

"Ask me what?" said Stephen genially, coming into the kitchen and going over to the sink to wash his hands. Caught again. It would be forever before she got away, and Cal and Captain Crunch would have left for lunch. Or gone sledding, or to deliver papers.

Julie leaned against the counter. So did Stephen. He was looking out toward the bird feeder. Was he really ready to listen to her?

"They're hungry, all right," he said. "It's good I got the sunflower seed." Then he looked back toward Julie. "What did you want to ask?" he said. "I have all afternoon."

I don't, thought Julie. "I wondered whether you'd help me with my math." she asked.

"Be glad to," Stephen answered, his eyes straying back toward the bird feeder. "Is there a problem you can't solve?"

"It's not that—" her mother began.

"I can explain, Mom," Julie interrupted. She felt crowded in by the adults in her life—Mom, Stephen, even her dad. She wanted to push them all away and get back into the space and freedom of the snowy out-of-doors.

"It's not one problem. It's all new, because I've changed schools."

"I see," said Stephen. "That's understandable."

"And I'm sure you could explain it all to me." Stephen looked pleased, as though Julie had said he was her favorite stepfather.

"I'm flattered, Julie, that you've asked me for help." He said it very formally. "And I want to do the right thing. It's been a long time since I was in seventh grade. What do they study in math these days?"

"Right now we're doing properties of equations in word problems."

"What are they talking about?" Stephen seemed irritated. "Properties of equations."

"That's what I'm trying to learn," Julie explained. This was going to take forever.

"Julie, math education has changed so much. Even the vocabulary. That's changed. I think you should be tutored for a few weeks by someone at school who's up on the latest methods. Then I can help you with any particular problems you have. You'll get off to a better start that way."

Julie knew her mother wouldn't say, "What did I tell you?" But there was still some humiliation in having her ask, "Want me to call the school?"

"I don't want to be tutored," said Julie. What use was a stepfather if he couldn't save you from being tutored in math?

"Yes, it would probably only be a few weeks." Julie thought Stephen was dismissing her because he went back to looking at the bird feeder. Then he added, "I'm sure you'd catch on quickly."

That was balm. Julie almost smiled at Stephen. But he didn't deserve it. They were all getting her to do what they wanted first and making her feel better about it afterward.

"I'll handle it," Julie said as she went over to the

refrigerator for an apple. Wasn't that what Mary told
her parents? She looked for an apple without any
spots. "I'm going outside again," she said as she
rinsed it off at the sink. She'd have to think of another
plan or else she'd have to endure being tutored. At the
moment it didn't seem half as important as getting
back to Cal and Captain Crunch—and Mr. Hawkins.

"Do you think it's safe for Julie to take the metro
alone?" she heard her mother ask Stephen as she left
to get her jacket. She stood in the hall to listen to his
answer.

"Sure," he said. "Kids her age do it all the time." He
probably wants to get rid of me for the day, she
thought. But she was pleased. She wanted to be able
to visit her dad on her own.

She hurried through the kitchen and outside to the
other world—the re-created, snow-covered world.

As she crossed the street, biting into her apple, she
looked toward Cal's house for any sign of life. There
was nobody in sight, except . . . . Well, there really was
somebody, after all. The gray-striped tabby cat with
white paws was sitting on the porch as though it belonged there. When it saw Julie, it started down the
path toward her.

"Is Cal still around?" she asked the cat as it nuzzled
her boots. Her teeth felt cold from biting into the
apple.

"Let's go see," she suggested. The cat followed her
along the driveway and then ran ahead carrying its tail
high above the frosty ground. "It seems awfully
quiet," she said to the cat, "as though nobody's here,
except," she said as they turned the corner, "Mr. Hawkins. Why, Mr. Hawkins, you're almost human," said

Julie. "Anyone would know you teach math." Cal and Captain Crunch had added a green baseball cap, prunes for eyes, and a carrot nose. His stick mouth looked appropriately severe. The cat went over as though to rub itself against Mr. Hawkins.

"He's a cold fish," said Julie, turning her apple to make sure she had bitten down to the core on every side. "But my boots aren't much better," she added as the cat came back to make a circuit of their shiny sides. She found a trash can at the corner of the house, where she put her apple core. Then she bent over and stroked the cat.

"Looks as though we're too late. We'll have to keep each other company," she said. She wondered where Cal and Captain Crunch were—inside having lunch or off somewhere else having fun in the snow.

"We have a lot in common," she said to the cat. "We don't belong anywhere. Either of us. I'd give you a home, but Stephen wouldn't. He hates . . . ." Julie heard the back door of Cal's house open and looked up. Cal was standing at the top of the steps.

"Hi, Jewel," he said. "What d'you think of Mr. Hawkins?"

"Very lifelike," said Julie. It was so easy to joke with Cal.

"You can have your scarf if . . ." said Cal.

"If what?" Julie asked.

"You help me deliver newspapers."

"Sure!" said Julie. "I'd like to. But how?" she asked, untwisting the scarf. Mr. Hawkins looked naked without it. "What do I need to do?"

"You pull the wagon," said Cal. "It's too deep for a bicycle and Mom thinks Captain Crunch has been

out in the cold long enough. So without you, I'd have
to keep running back to the wagon."

While Cal got an old red wagon out of the garage,
Julie shook the snow off her scarf and put it around her
neck. It was still very cold from having been worn by
Mr. Hawkins.

"You're a pal," said Cal as they took the wagon to
the curb where the newspapers had been left by the
delivery truck. Then they loaded it up, piling them as
high as they would go without sliding off. Cal put the
rest in a loose cloth bag, which he carried over his
shoulder.

"Let's see if we can break the record," he said as
they started off. "If you pull and I toss, it might be
possible."

"Who are you racing against this time?" said Julie.

"Just myself," said Cal. "It makes it more interesting. The fastest I've ever done it by wagon is seventy-
eight minutes."

Over an hour! That was a lot of walking.

Cal had a large digital watch that he used to keep
time. After each block of delivering papers, Cal would
look at it and say, "Right on time. It's faster with two,
but slower in the snow."

As they walked along, Julie thought she recognized
the area where she had gotten lost. "Is this where I
met you?" she asked Cal.

He was all business. "Yes, it is," he said. "And it
usually takes twelve minutes. Unless the German
shepherd's loose and starts to attack you."

"Then what do you do?" asked Julie.

"Threaten it with a stick." He picked one up from

the side of the street. "Not very big, but wave it if you see a German shepherd."

Cal took five newspapers and stuck them in his bag. As he was starting across the street, a large, short-haired, black and tan dog came running toward them, barking.

"There it is," said Cal. "There goes our time."

"That's all right," said Julie. "Go ahead. I'll take care of it."

"Great," said Cal. "I'll hurry."

"*Grff, rfff,*" growled the German shepherd. Its teeth were thick and yellow. Could they bite through boots? It seemed to be mobilizing for an attack. "*Rfff, rfff,*" it barked, lunging at Julie.

What have I promised? she thought, too scared to lift the stick. I don't know any more about dogs than I do about cats.

The German shepherd moved back and barked again. Julie wanted to run. She wanted to call Cal. But she remembered Captain Crunch with the cat and held herself completely still. Somewhere she'd heard that if you did that, dogs sniffed at you and went away. Besides, they were trying to break Cal's record and every second counted.

"*Rfff, rfff,*" barked the German shepherd. Then it closed its jaws with its teeth showing and subsided into growling. But it didn't seem interested in leaving. Maybe it was time for the stick and a firm command. Julie didn't think she could bear the strain of standing rigid much longer. The dog came toward her again, still growling.

"Go home," said Julie emphatically, ready to wave

the stick above her head. But the dog stopped growling and sniffed her boots. Then, as though disgusted
with what it found there, probably the smell of the cat,
it turned and went back down the street and into its
own yard.

"You're great," said Cal, running up. "You're
strong and brave like a real princess. Princess Jewel."

When they got to the end of the block, he checked
his watch. "Twelve minutes it is. There's still a chance.
As long as you keep the dogs out of our way."

"I hope there aren't any more," said Julie. She was
pleased with herself, but she didn't want to test her
courage further.

As they got close to the end of the route, they were
both running. Julie folded the papers to get them
ready for Cal. Then she ran along pulling the wagon
through the snowy street to catch up with him. If she
wasn't careful to pull it straight, it got off to the side
where the cars hadn't packed down the snow. "Just a
minute, Cal, I'm coming," she would call, jerking the
wagon back to the center.

When Cal finished his paper route, they were four
blocks from home. Cal checked his watch. "One hour
and eleven minutes. Right on schedule, but not
ahead," he said. "Still, if we hurry, there's a chance ..."

"I don't know whether I can make it," said Julie.
The backs of her legs ached from walking and the
hand that held the wagon was so numb she wasn't sure
she was still holding it.

"Don't give up, Jewel. I'll pull you in the wagon."

"No, that would really slow us down. Wait just a
minute while I change hands."

"Well, at least I'll pull the wagon. If we don't break the record this time, we can do it another time." Cal sounded disappointed.

Julie started to run down the center of the street and Cal panted after her with the wagon.

"Okay, Jewel," he called, "that's the spirit." She was breathless, but her hands got warmer and her legs stopped aching.

When they reached Cal's house, the cat was sitting like a judge on the steps waiting to greet them. "Did we win?" said Cal to the cat. "Maybe. That was," he said, pushing his jacket sleeve back from his watch, "seventy-six and a half minutes. That's a minute and a half less. Of course it wasn't quite fair because we ran, but then we had the snow. But we set a new record for sure. You're a wonder, Jewel!"

Me, a wonder. Julie sat down on the wagon remembering how defeated she had been feeling earlier that afternoon.

"Next time it snows," said Cal, "we'll try to set another record."

"I'd like to," said Julie. She wished she could do it every day.

"Looks as though I'll be able to bicycle tomorrow," said Cal.

"In the snow?"

"If it's packed down and they plow the street."

"I guess we'll have school." Together they looked over to the west, where the deep, cold red of an unseen sun setting behind snow-covered houses and trees promised an ordinary school day.

"'Fraid so," said Cal.

"Then I'd better do my math homework." Julie

stood up. Her jeans weren't very heavy and she was
beginning to feel the cold of the metal wagon. Since
Cal already thought she was a wonder, she didn't care
if he asked her how she was doing in math. It would
be a relief to talk to someone her own age about it.

"You'd better," Cal said, "or Mr. Hawkins will de-
vour you alive. Especially since you took away your
scarf."

Julie thought of asking Cal to help her with math,
but he had probably forgotten it or would find properties of equations beneath his dignity. Although Mrs.
Barker did say she could be tutored by a student. If
that was what she chose, maybe it would be Cal.

"Maybe I'll see you at school," she said.

"I doubt it," said Cal. Julie felt rebuffed. "Don't
forget," Cal continued. "Ninth graders are invisible."
This time he didn't look as though he was joking.

"So long," said Julie.

"Thanks for helping." Cal picked up the handle and
pulled the red wagon down the driveway behind him.

Julie crossed the street slowly. She hated to go inside even though it was starting to get dark. She'd find
Mom and Stephen sitting on the couch close together
and she'd feel like an intruder. "How was it? What've
you been doing?" they'd say, trying to seem interested
when she'd know they really wanted to be alone.

"Yoo-hoo. Yoo-hoo, little girl." Was someone calling her? Impossible! It was a long time since she'd
been a little girl. Still, she looked around through the
dusky shadows. The lights were on at her house, but
there was no one outside.

"Yoo-hoo." She looked across the street. No one on
Cal's porch. Or did she see the silent silhouette of the

cat? Then she looked the other way and saw, of all
things, a figure on Mrs. Mitchell's porch beckoning to
her. Should she go? Was it safe? Should she pretend
not to hear? There was no one around to rescue her
if she needed it.

Don't be dumb, Julie told herself. She's only a flesh-
and-blood old lady, not a ghost. So she crossed the
street and walked up the front path to Mrs. Mitchell's
porch. But when she got there, she wished she hadn't
come. Mrs. Mitchell, leaning on a cane and lit up by
the lanterns at her door, looked exactly as Captain
Crunch had described her. Everything about her was
pointy—even her eyes, which seemed to be nothing
more than sharp little black drills coming right at her.

"Were you the one?" Mrs. Mitchell said. Her voice
cutting through the cold evening air was sharp too,
but it didn't sound unkind. Even so, Julie felt guilty.

"What? Me?" said Julie.

"The path," said Mrs. Mitchell. She waved toward
it with her cane. As Julie looked down at the path, she
saw Mrs. Mitchell's feet. Not feet with shoes, but feet
with bedroom slippers and white socks. A long, faded,
blue flannel nightgown hung down below Mrs. Mitchell's old black winter coat.

"Well, did you?" Mrs. Mitchell said.

"Yes," said Julie, "with Cal, down the street." It
seemed only fair to mention that Cal had helped. Or
would she be getting him into trouble?

"Thank you, dahling," Mrs. Mitchell said. Julie was
surprised at the warmth in the abrasive old voice.
"You must be a nice girl, the way Cal's a nice boy. He
always stays at his own place." What did that mean?
That she didn't want her path shoveled after all? "I've

never chased him out of my garden. Trampling down
daffodil shoots and crocuses."

"Oh, I'm sure he wouldn't, and I wouldn't either."
I wouldn't dare go into your garden, she thought. The
front walk was all right because one could get away
quickly, but the garden was probably full of vines and
prickly shrubs that grabbed onto one and held tight.

"You've got a pretty mamma." Mrs. Mitchell's voice
was boring further in. Would she ask about her father?
Julie wished she could find a way to leave.

"I'm sorry I don't have anything to give you, dahling."

"Give me?" said Julie.

"For shoveling the path. I don't get out much. But
I just love people."

"That's all right. It was fun," Julie said.

"You tell Cal Winston thank you."

"I will," Julie said. "Tomorrow. If I see him."

"Let me know when I can do anything for you."
Mrs. Mitchell had opened her front door. Julie looked
past her into the shadowy clutter of the front hall. It
was dark except for a rose-colored globe way at the
end. She could see clusters of dark shapes standing
ready like evil spirits to reach out and catch her.

"And come visit me some time."

Never, never, Julie thought to herself.

In the doorway, Mrs. Mitchell turned around, leaning on her cane. Julie could see the bristles on her
chin. She could smell the warm, musty air in the dark
rooms behind the bent old lady.

"I'll pray for you, dahling," she said and closed the
door.

Thank you? Julie didn't know how she would have responded if there'd been time. Praying for her? She had that strange feeling again, the feeling of magic and religion mixed up together. Of someone saying a spell over her when she wasn't sure she wanted it said. She looked up above the closed door.

ARE YOU SAVED?

She knew what the sign said even though it was too dark to read it. What did she need to be saved from? She still hadn't thought of an answer. From having things happen that she couldn't control—her father leaving, her mom marrying Stephen? It was too late to be saved from them.

Julie felt she could stand right there and cry over those parts of her life that could no longer be saved. And Mrs. Mitchell would open the door again and find her crying. And she'd call her "dahling" again, which would be comforting. And invite her in again . . . .

I'd better leave, Julie thought, before she comes back. Quickly, she looked for the picture of the young shepherd. He was still there in the golden lantern light, holding the little lamb in his arms. And he would be, Julie thought, as long as Mrs. Mitchell was there. Clearly, she never took cards down. Even when they were too weathered to be legible, she must have known what was written on them.

"Like a shepherd he careth for thee," Julie said to herself as she walked home. I'd care for a baby lamb, too, Julie thought. She could imagine the feel of its tight curls. Once long ago, she'd fed a baby lamb with a bottle. Once when her mom and dad had taken her to visit a farm.

As she started up her own driveway, she had a sense of blackness behind her. She looked back toward Mrs. Mitchell's. The lights on the porch had been turned off. Though she hadn't wanted to linger there, now that the house appeared closed away from her, she felt rejected.

"Pussy," she whispered over toward Cal's porch, "where are you?" Calling, she thought, from one stray to the other. Nothing moved. Had it found a place to spend the night? Was someone feeding it? If it was a stray, she wanted to do something to help the cat. She'd talk it over with Cal when she told him about seeing Mrs. Mitchell. That is, if she could find the invisible ninth-grade boy.

The Invisible Boy

By the time Julie left for school, her mother and Stephen had already been gone for half an hour. They had gotten off in a flurry of scraping, brushing, and defrosting two cars.

"You're lucky, Julie," Stephen had said, stamping the snow off his shoes as he came back into the kitchen for a final gulp of coffee. "You're lucky to be able to walk."

I'd be a lot luckier, Julie thought as she chased the last few Rice Krispies around her cereal bowl, if I could tell Mrs. Barker you were going to help me with my math. On the other hand, why should Stephen want to spend the time? If he'd been her real father . . . . That was an idea. Maybe her real father could help her. When she was smaller, he used to help her with things like fractions and long division. He wouldn't really understand the new ways of doing things. He'd get her to explain it and tell her she was a genius. Julie wondered how much he knew about properties of equations in word problems. There wasn't any more time to think about it now. She had to make her peanut butter and jelly sandwich and put it in the tote bag along with her books and her math homework. Finished. Maybe all wrong, but it was finished.

When she stepped out the back door, breathless with the rush of getting ready and the shock of the cold

air, she saw the cat. Not the yellow cat that Stephen
was always chasing. Not the cat that killed birds. She
saw the stray. The gray-striped tabby cat with white
paws sitting in the middle of the brick patio where the
snow had been brushed away, switching its tail back
and forth.

It ran over to Julie as she stood for a moment pulling on her mittens and gave its usual friendly nudge.
"I'm glad you made it through the night," said Julie.
"But this is a dangerous place to be. If Stephen had
seen you, you wouldn't still be here," Julie said to the
cat. "You'd have been scared out of all nine of your
lives."

As Julie hurried down the driveway, the cat ran
along with her. "Maybe we'll see Cal," she said to the
cat. "And we can tell him about Mrs. Mitchell." She
looked over at his house. All was closed and silent.
There were no cars in the driveway. But in the hard-
packed snow down the driveway and along the street,
she thought she saw the thin imprint of a bicycle tire.

"I guess he's left already." The cat was looking up
at her as though waiting for an answer. Was this the
way it was going to be all day? That she would keep
seeing where Cal had been without ever actually seeing Cal?

"It's a lot of nonsense," she said to the cat, who was
leading the way along the narrow path through the
snow, "about ninth graders being invisible. I'll find
this one before the day is over."

"Hi, honey!" Cynthia was waiting at the end of the
tarmac path that led from Raymond Street to the
crossing at East-West Highway. "Can you wait? Rosalie should be here any minute."

"Sure," said Julie. Why not take a chance? The snow had probably made everyone forget about report cards anyhow.

"It's mighty cold," said Cynthia, stamping her boots and startling the cat, which had been on the verge of becoming acquainted with them. "I have to make sure my feet are still there." The cat streaked back down the cleared sidewalk toward Julie's house and disappeared up her driveway.

"But with the sun . . . ." said Julie. It was still just a rosy promise in the early morning sky. "When it's up."

"I'll finally get warm," said Cynthia. "In history I have a seat by the window. Right in the sun. After lunch. And it's so warm and the class is so boring—" Cynthia yawned.

"That you fall asleep." Julie laughed.

"Right," said Cynthia. "By the way," she continued, as though what she was going to say was related, "I saw Cal Winston go past on his bicycle."

Julie knew the feeling for what it was the moment she had it. Jealousy! That's what came of getting involved with boys. There was no way that tumbled black curls under a red tam'oshanter could compete with sleek, straight, long, blond hair under a blue pom-pom hat.

"Did he say anything?" Julie asked. If he did, it meant that he didn't really act as though ninth graders were invisible. Not when he didn't want to.

"No, he was too busy trying not to slip all over the place on his bicycle."

"Who's 'he'?" Rosalie came up as Cynthia was talking.

"Julie's friend, Cal Winston."

"Oh, we've been trying to get to know him for ages," said Rosalie. "And you've just moved in. You are a fast worker."

The girls took so much for granted that wasn't true. As though she and Cal were already going together or something. It was ridiculous when yesterday was the longest she'd ever spent with a boy ever, except for her cousins during the summer.

"She's a little ole black-eyed Susan that boys can't resist," teased Cynthia. They were waiting for the signal from the traffic control to cross East-West Highway.

"How'd you do it?" said Rosalie. Well, at least she wasn't asking about her report card. But it was hard to answer. To be quite honest, she hadn't done anything. And she might not see Cal again. He might be invisible forevermore.

Yet, she wanted them to like her. "I didn't do anything," she said evasively.

Rosalie's laugh made the girls who were walking ahead of them look back. "Miss Modesty," she said.

They were close to school now. Julie looked over the groups of kids converging on the school or standing by the door talking or having snowball fights. No sign of Cal. She looked at the bicycles chained to the rack. She wouldn't know his bicycle, even if it was there, because she'd only seen it in the dark.

As they got to the door, the first bell rang, and everybody around them started pushing and shoving into the building.

"See you later, honey," said Cynthia in the crush.

"Stay out of trouble," said Rosalie.

I have some friends, now, thought Julie as she pushed through the crowded hall to her locker. But it was worrisome, because maybe it all depended on Cal. Maybe everything depended on whether Cal kept on being nice to her.

The homeroom teacher read the daily bulletin out loud. There was a long list of students who were supposed to see their guidance counselors "without fail—before the end of the school day." Julie's name was on the list.

"What'd you do?" asked Mary. "Or what didn't you do?" Her speech was slurred because she was putting on lipstick.

"It's only from changing schools," said Julie, which was the truth. Mary probably wouldn't be at all shocked by a C-minus. But Julie wasn't going to tell anyone, not *anyone* about it.

When the bell rang for the first class, Julie went out into the hall hoping that as she was levitated through the crowded hall toward her French room she would hear a voice in her ear saying, "Remember, Jewel, ninth graders are invisible."

Maybe, she thought later as she tried to give her attention to the verbs conjugated with *avoir* and those with *être,* she would see Cal when she went upstairs for math. That was where the ninth-grade lockers were and the ninth-grade lounge. Before she had math, though, she had history and then a free period when she ought to talk with Mrs. Barker. Now that her name was in the bulletin, the whole school knew she was going. There was no point in trying to do that part of it secretly. But she still hoped for a reprieve from the tutoring, some way to avoid being labeled as "dumb."

"Did you enjoy your snow day?" Mrs. Barker was wearing a dark-blue woolen suit with a round gold pin on the lapel and sensible, low-heeled shoes. Julie thought she smelled lavender as Mrs. Barker walked past her to close out the noise in the hall. Julie was glad the door was closed so nobody outside could hear.

"What did you do?" Mrs. Barker asked as she sat down behind her desk.

"We shoveled," said Julie, "and built a snowman." And met Cal and Captain Crunch, she thought, but didn't say.

"And didn't worry about math, I hope." It was easy for Mrs. Barker to smile and look reassuring. It wasn't really her problem. "And what did your parents say?" she continued. She said it so naturally. Like last time. Even though Julie was sure she knew, she acted as though nothing about Julie's home life was strange or different as far as she was concerned. Unless it was to Julie. And it was. And it was difficult not being able to talk to someone about it. And Mrs. Barker was there smiling, looking relaxed and sympathetic. The door was closed. She had a whole free period ahead of her.

"They're not really my parents," Julie said. "I mean he isn't."

"I know," said Mrs. Barker. "You don't think of a stepfather that way. Not at first, anyhow."

How could she introduce her new plan, her last hope of escape from being tutored at school? If she could talk frankly with Mrs. Barker, maybe Mrs. Barker would let her try it.

"Stephen—that's my stepfather—wouldn't help

me," said Julie. As she said it, Julie had the feeling that she was revealing a terrible brutality. Why wouldn't Stephen help her? It sounded awful. But Mrs. Barker took the news calmly.

"In what way wouldn't he help you?" she asked.

"With my math," Julie said, "with learning what I haven't been taught before."

"You wanted him to?" Mrs. Barker asked.

"Yes," said Julie. "So I wouldn't need to be tutored at school. And then I thought of . . . it might work. Asking my father. My real father."

"He lives in the area?"

"Yes."

"How often do you see him?"

"I used to see him all the time. But now we've moved. And he's moved. I'm going to see him this Saturday and ask him then."

Mrs. Barker didn't say anything for a minute. She sat back in her chair, looking out the window. There wasn't much to see. Some blue sky and the other wing of the school with snow piled up on the windowsills. The expression on Mrs. Barker's face didn't tell Julie anything.

She's probably thinking, How'm I going to handle this kid from a broken home so she doesn't become a mental case? Julie wished she hadn't said anything about Stephen and made herself conspicuous. Except she would be, if she got tutored. So there she was, in a box.

"Suppose we do this," said Mrs. Barker, leaning forward with her elbows on her desk and looking straight at Julie. "Suppose we set things up for you to be tutored here at school, but if, after talking with your father on Saturday, you want to cancel out, simply come and tell me on Monday morning."

"Would . . . would anyone know?" Julie whispered.

Mrs. Barker nodded her head as if to say that now she understood.

"Not until Monday," she said. "But let's plan how it would be. Did your parents have any opinion?"

Julie shook her head. "We didn't talk about it anymore," she said.

"I think you should try working with a ninth grader. We have one who's good at math and good at teaching and he likes helping other students. And you're bright. It won't take you long to catch on."

Oh! Julie could have hugged Mrs. Barker for that. At least she knew that Julie wasn't dumb. Maybe she'd tell everyone in the school. Maybe word would get around that although Julia M. Howard was being tutored, she wasn't dumb.

"Let's see." Mrs. Barker pulled two folders out of her file. "You have this period, third period . . . ." She looked at the other folder. "No, that won't work." She looked so disappointed that Julie found herself wanting it to work even though she didn't want to be tutored.

"Oh, here we are." She showed Julie the two schedules. "Monday, Wednesday, Thursday, sixth period. When you don't have P.E."

Julie saw the name at the top of the other schedule. Arnold Finch. Suppose it had been Cal Winston? It wouldn't be much help if Cal was invisible. She found herself smiling at the thought. An invisible tutor. Mrs. Barker thought she was smiling about Arnold.

"You know him already?" she asked.

"No," said Julie. A ninth grader. Not what she wanted. But better than a teacher. Anyone seeing them working together might think they were friends, special friends, rather than student and tutor.

The bell rang. The end of the period so soon! Julie and Mrs. Barker both stood up.

"If you don't cancel," she said, going over to open the door and then coming back to put her arm around Julie, "sixth period. In the conference room. It's very quiet and private. You'll like Arnold too. He's good at explaining things."

"Thanks," said Julie. What was she thanking Mrs. Barker for?

"Stop in and see me," said Mrs. Barker, "and let me know how things are going. You seem to be doing splendidly."

"Thanks," said Julie again, and hurried to her math class. The crazy guy, the one she had seen when she got her report, brushed past her as she went in. He was carrying a calculator on top of his books and had about twenty pencils in the pocket of his shirt.

"Do you agree?" he said as he passed. "Is Hawkins a nerd?"

"But why?" she started to ask him. He was already gone. There's someone else I sort of know, she thought as she took her usual seat, the desk that had a penciled heart with E loves W inside it. Despite her difficulties with math, she was starting to feel more at home in the school.

"You've arranged to get help?" Mr. Hawkins asked as Julie left the class. Julie looked around. There was no one near enough to overhear.

"Yes," she said, anxious to get away before anyone came.

"Good," he said. "The longer you wait, the harder it is to catch up."

"Yes," said Julie. He seemed to want to talk, but she didn't feel comfortable with him, even though she and Cal had made him into a snowman and he had worn her red scarf. He looked a bit like the snowman, now that she thought of it, short with a bald head.

"And Julie," he called after her as she started out the door, "don't be afraid to ask questions in class."

"Okay," said Julie. But she was. Who wanted to make a public display of ignorance?

Was that Cal's back she glimpsed at the end of the hall? People kept getting in her way so she couldn't see clearly. Besides, she'd never seen him without a cap, so she didn't know what his hair was like. Before she could catch up with the person who might be Cal, he had pushed through the double doors and started downstairs. When she got to the stairs, no one was going down. Everyone was coming up. Whoever it was had disappeared. Cal was doing a good job of being invisible.

Did Cal mean he was invisible at school, but not at home? As Julie got the books from her locker at the end of the day, she planned to hurry back and catch him before he began delivering newspapers. He might want Julie to help with the wagon again after all. According to Cynthia, it had been slippery in the morning. And she needed to talk with him about the cat and Mrs. Mitchell and see what the snowman looked like after a day of melting. She might even lend Mr. Hawkins her red scarf since he'd been nice to her in school. The air was so much warmer now, she'd hardly need it.

Julie thought she wouldn't wait for Cynthia and Rosalie. It would be easier to talk with Cal alone. But when she stood at the top of the school steps, wondering how she would get through the frenzy of snowballs beneath her, Rosalie ran up and grabbed her arm.

"Come on," she said, "we've got to make a dash for it." She dragged Julie after her. "Cynthia's over there," she said, ducking to avoid a snowball, "hiding from Tony." They headed down the front path toward the street. As they reached the other side of the melee, Julie felt the soft explosion of a snowball on her back. It might have been Cal. She looked around and saw the boy from the advanced math class.

"Guess who else is a nerd," she called back. Rosalie was still pulling her along.

"Cynthia's hiding behind the green car," she said. They went around to the other side of the car. Cynthia was leaning against it.

"Let's go," said Rosalie, and they crossed the street together.

"Gotcha," said a kid popping out from behind a tree to dump a big, messy snowball on top of Cynthia's pom-pom hat and run back toward school.

"Tony Marshall, that's no way for a gentleman to act," said Cynthia. Even after brushing the snow off her hat and out of her hair, Cynthia seemed perfectly groomed and composed.

She's glamorous and I'm not, thought Julie. Not a bit. She didn't see how anyone—Cal for instance—

could help but prefer Cynthia, or Rosalie too, with her vivacious manner. If she saw Cal, she would much rather see him alone.

They hadn't gone far, sliding their boots through the slush, when they started talking about Cal.

"Did you have lunch with him?" Rosalie asked.

"Will you introduce us?" asked Cynthia.

"We'll be your friends forever," said Rosalie, giving one of her laughs.

"We'd be your friends forever, honey," said Cynthia, "even if there wasn't any Cal Winston."

Have lunch with Cal! She wasn't even sure that she'd seen his back at a distance. "Do you know who Arnold Finch is?" Julie wanted to change the subject and she was curious. She hoped they wouldn't ask her why she wanted to know. Cynthia looked surprised.

"How do you know him?" she asked.

"I heard his name," said Julie, which was the truth.

"He isn't a kid," said Rosalie, "he's pure brain. He's the brain that threw the snowball at you."

Her tutor! That kid! Well, at least she knew what he looked like, if worse came to worse.

Together they turned down Raymond Street. Rosalie was going home with Cynthia to listen to records.

"Wanta come?" Cynthia asked. Julie did, but she wanted to see Cal more.

"Can I come another time?" said Julie.

"Any day, honey," said Cynthia.

" 'I wonder why, he's so shy,' " hummed Rosalie. "We know," she said.

As she looked down along the street, Julie could see Cal's bicycle at the foot of his steps, loaded with newspapers, but no sign of Cal. I'll wait till they've gone on and then I'll talk to him, she decided.

They were passing Mrs. Mitchell's house. The branches of the guardian evergreens, relieved of their burden of snow, had sprung back up. The afternoon sunlight slanted in on the front door and the graying placards around it. The house looked quite different from the day before, still mysterious, but as though the magic was friendly magic.

"There's Cal," said Rosalie.

Now what shall I do? thought Julie. What shall I do about Cynthia and Rosalie?

Captain Crunch had come out with Cal and was holding his bicycle while he stuffed the last newspapers into the baskets. Without looking toward Julie, Cal took hold of the handlebars, swung his leg over the center, and, calling "Good-bye Crunch," started off.

"Cal!" Julie ran toward him. She wanted to see him so badly. After looking for him all day.

Not seeming to hear her, Cal rode a little way down the pavement and made a sharp turn out of the driveway.

"Cal!" Julie called again. At that moment, the bicycle skidded in the slush. Julie saw Cal suspended above his bike, still holding onto the handlebars like a reckless stunt man trying to do handstands. Then Cal flew one way and his bike another.

For a minute, nothing moved. The bike lay in a snowbank at the side of the street, while near the center Cal was sprawled in a puddle of melting snow. It was only a minute. Then Julie dropped her books by the steps and started running again. So did Captain Crunch. Together they ran out into the street, in spite of the big, black car that was coming. Julie hoped that she was protecting Cal with her presence, warning the car that he was there.

Because of the snow, the car came down the street slowly. Julie saw it stop, barely touching Cal's cap, which had landed several feet from where Cal was lying.

"Cal!" She knelt down beside him. He wasn't really lying on the ground. He was resting on his elbows and knees, and as she knelt by him he turned and sat down at the edge of the puddle.

"Where's my bike?" he said. The car door banged.

"You all right, dear?" A lady with gray hair, wearing a hat and gloves and galoshes and a black coat with a fur collar, came toward them, holding Cal's cap. She was the driver of the car.

"Yeah, I'm okay," said Cal. "Where's my bike?"

"Over here!" Captain Crunch started to pull the bike out of the snowbank. "Help!" he said. "It's stuck!"

"Hold my books," Julie heard Rosalie tell Cynthia. She saw her go over to help Captain Crunch. Julie hadn't even noticed that they were waiting on the sidewalk behind her.

"It's fortunate I was driving slowly," said the lady in a bright, piping voice. "Do you think this is a good day for bicycling, dear?" she said to Cal, who was gradually standing up as though something might break off, if he wasn't careful.

"Boys," said the lady cheerfully. "I spent hours in

the emergency room with mine. Of course they have boys of their own now."

"How's my bike?" asked Cal, cautiously straightening one leg and then the other.

"Cal, your jeans are ripped," said Julie.

"And there's blood," said Captain Crunch.

"You aren't dizzy, are you?" said the lady.

Cal thought for a minute. "No, I'm okay," he said.

"What about the blood?" said Julie.

"Just scrapes," said Cal, bending over to check. He took a step or two toward the bicycle. "It can't be much," he said. "I can walk, and I've got to deliver the papers." He limped over and took the bike from Captain Crunch and Rosalie.

"Here," said Julie. "Let me help you brush off the newspapers."

"Well, you don't need us anymore," said Rosalie, getting her books from Cynthia and looking meaningfully at Julie.

"Thanks," said Julie. "See you," she called as they started down the street.

"Tomorrow, honey," Cynthia called back with her pom-pom swinging over her shoulder.

"Didn't you notice Cynthia and Rosalie?" Julie asked Cal as she and Captain Crunch brushed snow off the newspapers while Cal held the bike.

"Yeah, I saw them," said Cal.

"You acted as though they didn't exist."

"I'm still invisible," he said. Julie looked up at him and laughed.

"For someone who's invisible, you just attracted an awful lot of attention," she said. Cal laughed too.

"Cal's good at magic," said Captain Crunch.

"I always said that if my boys could laugh, I knew they were all right," said the lady. "Here's your hat, dear."

"Thanks a lot," said Cal and put it on.

He has curls, Julie thought as he pulled it down over his ears. Now I'll know what I'm looking for at school.

"Don't be foolish," said the lady, "but of course you will. And wash your knees when you get home."

"Thanks," said Cal. "I'll be really careful this time."

"And if you wouldn't mind moving," the lady piped on, "I'm going to pull over there and leave a pink begonia with my friend, Mrs. Mitchell."

Aha! Julie and Cal looked at each other.

"She can't get out much in the winter, you know."

It took them a while to get the snow shaken out of the newspapers.

"I'm afraid it'll melt," said Cal, "and get them all wet."

While they were working, Julie tried to catch a glimpse of Mrs. Mitchell. Was she still wearing her nightgown? But when the door was answered, the lady with the black coat went inside and Julie couldn't see the person standing in the shadows.

"I could pull the wagon," Julie suggested.

"No, I'll make it," said Cal.

"Your jeans are wet," said Julie. "Aren't your legs cold?"

"Yes, but I'm late," said Cal. He wheeled his bike out to the center of the street before he got onto it. "Good-bye Crunch," he said. "Good-bye Jewel. Why don't you visit Mr. Hawkins. He's lonely."

Julie watched Cal cycle off, much more slowly than before.

"Wanta see Mr. Hawkins?" said Captain Crunch.

"Sure," said Julie. She wished she could find an excuse to stay around till Cal came back. But that would be a long time.

"Yoo-hoo, little girl!"

"Who's that?" said Captain Crunch.

"Mrs. Mitchell. I talked to her yesterday. Wanta come see her?" asked Julie.

"No. And don't you go, Julie. Cal says she's magic."

"That's all right. It's nice magic." Julie patted him on the head. "I'll be back."

Mrs. Mitchell was standing on the porch talking with her friend. The same old blue nightgown did indeed hang down beneath her coat. Maybe she got dressed at night and wore her nightgown during the day, Julie speculated. Since witches were busiest at night.

"Is he all right?" demanded Mrs. Mitchell.

She must mean Cal, Julie decided. "He said he was."

"I'm glad," said Mrs. Mitchell. "That was a dreadful fall." Had she seen it happen? Did she stand behind the curtains in the dusky dining room watching all that happened in the street?

"This your cat?" said Mrs. Mitchell's friend. The gray-striped tabby cat had appeared from nowhere. Maybe it was magic. It stood with its back arched, looking as much like a witch's cat as possible. Then it rubbed itself against the lady's galoshes.

"It's a stray, I think," said Julie.

Mrs. Mitchell's friend bent over to pat it. "Too bad," she said, "such an affectionate pussy."

"If it's a stray," said Mrs. Mitchell, "you should give
it a home."

"I wish I could," said Julie, "But . . . ." Stephen.
Everywhere she turned, she seemed to run into a bar-
rier named Stephen.

"Well, good-bye, Lucy," said Mrs. Mitchell's friend.
A witch named Lucy! That would amuse Cal.

"I'll tell Cal Winston you asked," said Julie. She
wanted to get away before there were more difficult
questions or explanations.

"Tell him to be sensible," said Mrs. Mitchell's
friend. "Not that it'll help."

Julie found Captain Crunch back with Mr. Hawkins.
Mr. Hawkins had suffered a considerable weight loss.
A day of melting snow had left him looking drained
and porous.

"Let's make another," said Captain Crunch.

"The snow's too wet," said Julie, "and there isn't
enough. Besides, I have to go home."

"Cal said it might snow on Saturday. Then we can
go sledding."

"I won't be here," said Julie.

"Why not?"

"I have to visit someone." Julie almost wished it
would snow too hard for her to go. She might want to
do something with Cal, or Cynthia and Rosalie.

No, that wasn't what she wanted. She wanted to see
her real father and ask him about math. And she
wanted to travel on the metro—alone and independent. What did she want? It didn't matter. Since she
never seemed to have any choice about what she did.
Since everything always got decided for her.

Lindsay

It's just as well, thought Julie, looking between Mom's head and Stephen's head out the front window of the car at the WTOP sign on the back of the bus they were following. No one—Cal, or Cynthia and Rosalie—had suggested doing something on Saturday, so it was just as well she was going to the zoo with her father. Otherwise, it would have been the usual boring Saturday, hanging around the house and feeling like a third wheel with Mom and Stephen.

She could smell the bus exhaust being pulled in through their car heater. It would be better to ride the bus than follow it. If this was the bus that connected with the metro, she might as well have taken it.

"Later," Mom turned around to say, "when you're used to the metro, you can take this bus—you catch it across from school—and ride the whole way by yourself. But remember," she said, looking as though she still hadn't gotten used to the idea of sending Julie off on the metro alone, "don't speak to strangers."

While Stephen waited in the car, Mom showed Julie how to feed the fare card machine a dollar bill, facing the way it did in the picture.

"You do it yourself," she said. The machine sucked in Julie's dollar and coughed up a fare card.

"You use this to get in," said Mom.

Julie stuck the fare card into the turnstile. Nothing happened.

"Follow the picture." Her mother was frowning.

"I'll do it all right, Mom," said Julie. "Don't worry." She turned the card around and this time the turnstile sprang open.

"Sorry," said her mother with an apologetic smile. "I know you'll be okay. But call me from the zoo, will you, sweetheart?"

"Sure, Mom."

"Good-bye," said Mom. "Have a good time."

That was nice of her. Julie had read in "Dear Abby" about a kid who always had to pretend she'd had a horrible time when she went to visit her father. Otherwise, her mother got jealous.

Mom stayed and watched her go up on the escalator. Julie waved. "Good-bye," she called.

And then she couldn't see her anymore. Dear Mom. She had looked very lonely. But of course she had Stephen in the car. Still, Julie wished she could run back and hug her.

As she reached the platform, she saw a train waiting. But she restrained the impulse to hurry into it before it left. Not many people were getting on, while there were a lot of people standing on the other side of the platform. SILVER SPRING, it said on the front. It went the wrong way, then. This must be the right train coming from the opposite direction. The lights on the edge of the platform blinked as it neared the station. VAN NESS. That was right. Julie got on, feeling pleased that she had figured it all out.

Since it was Saturday, the car wasn't too crowded,

so it was easy to get a seat by the window. Julie hoped no one would sit next to her. Then there would be less danger of speaking to strangers, which could be a problem if strangers spoke to you.

FORT TOTTEN. BROOKLAND. Julie noticed the name of each stop, even though she wasn't getting off till the end. Any minute it might rain or snow, thought Julie, looking out at the gray sky. Even so she felt lighthearted. She loved the smooth surge of the train between stops. She loved looking down from above at the maze of city streets and the poky cars.

After Rhode Island Avenue, the metro sped confidently on through a network of train tracks and then went underground at Union Station. Now it was dark between stops. Nothing to look at. With mixed feelings of anticipation and awkwardness, Julie started to think about her father. She'd seen so little of him lately, and her life had changed so much. JUDICIARY SQUARE, GALLERY PLACE. The train hurried her along as though on an urgent mission—carrying Julie to her real father.

At the end of the line the train stopped in an emphatic way and everyone got off. After taking the escalator up to the next level, Julie joined the line at the exit turnstile. She put her fare card in the slot. Oops, wrong way again. Then she took another escalator up to the street level. Dad had said he would meet her right at the top of the escalator. Would he be on time? Would she have to wait and worry about whether he was coming?

He would forget. Julie suddenly felt certain of it. At the very least, he would be late. He always was when he and Mom were married. Maybe that had been the problem. Stephen was always on time. But when her father did come, it was like music, like the polka record he used to play, and they'd dance together, hopping and twirling to the antics of the clarinet.

There was no one waiting at the top of the escalator. Julie tightened her scarf and put her mittens on. She hoped she didn't have to call her father. It would be embarrassing to listen to his excuses. Or suppose he didn't answer. What an awful feeling of emptiness that would give her. Which direction would he come from? She looked where she thought his apartment was. Would he be walking or driving? How far away was the zoo? She really didn't know anything about where she was, just somewhere on Connecticut Avenue.

And I know how to get home, she reminded herself. At first she hadn't cared a whole lot about going to the zoo, but now she thought she would be really disappointed to miss it. And to have Stephen and Mom surprised and sympathetic if she got home early. The thought was as dismal as the dampness surging up from the subway below and descending from the clouds above to meet precisely at the spot where she stood.

Julie felt gloved hands over her eyes. "Boo," someone whispered in her ear. Then he kissed her on the cheek.

"Daddy!" Julie swung around. "Daddy!" She put her arms about his neck and kissed him on his own nice, scratchy cheek. She sniffed the piney fragrance of his shaving lotion.

"You smell right," she said.

"That's what all the ladies tell me." Her father gave her a big squeeze. "I parked around the corner," he said. "I wanted to be here before you, but the car doesn't like cold weather."

"Did it stall?" asked Julie. That was one thing that hadn't changed.

"It's all right now," said Dad, guiding her to the car and holding the door for her, "now that it's warmed up." It took him a few minutes to maneuver out of the parking space. "My apartment's that way, north," he said as they waited at the light. "You'll have to come see it when it's all fixed up."

"I could help," Julie volunteered.

"I'll bet you could," he said. "If we have time after the zoo, you can look it over. And the zoo's this way," he continued, turning down Connecticut Avenue. "Shall we park by the elephants or the ducks?"

"Elephants," said Julie. "And giraffes."

"All right," he said, "we'll park at the top and roll slowly down to the bottom."

"Then how will we get back to the car?" asked Julie.

"By camel," said her dad.

Julie was waiting for him to ask her about school. Then she would say, "It's okay. But I need some help with math." That would be the easiest way. Otherwise, she'd have to introduce the subject, clearing her throat and saying, "Dad, I wanted to ask you something."

They were pulling into the parking lot now, only a step from the elephant house.

"Julie." Dad cleared his throat. "I wanted to tell you . . . . You aren't hungry?" he asked.

"I haven't thought about it," said Julie.

"A friend of mine wanted to meet us for lunch, but she can't get here until one o'clock."

"That's okay," said Julie. Even when it wasn't. Not a bit okay. She didn't want to eat lunch with a stranger. Someone Dad would be fussing over and listening to when he should be listening to Julie. Who'd say she was sweet (they always did) when she felt like a lemon inside. And how would she ask Dad about her math with this "friend" hanging onto him? Julie would have liked to leave. Walk away from her father out of the zoo, back Connecticut Avenue to the metro and then the bus, and then her mom and Stephen . . . . No, not that either.

"It's not such a great day," said Julie, opening the door of the warm car to the devouring cold. In fact, no one would think of coming to the zoo on a day like this except parents and kids who only saw each other on Saturdays and didn't know what else to do.

"Shall we start with the elephants?" Dad said, turning his coat collar up around his neck. *"Brrr,"* he said. "It's a perfect day for polar bears. That's where I told Lindsay we'd meet her," he rattled on. He seemed to sense the chill emanating from Julie as much as from the air.

Lindsay. She sounded like someone out of *True Romance.* An actress, a model. Very proper with a name like Lindsay, but very beautiful. Someone who'll make me feel insignificant, thought Julie.

"She wants to get to know you," said her father as he held open the door to the elephant house. It was warm and smelly inside, the smell of hay and manure and big animal bodies. It might sound as though Dad was about to get married too, but Julie knew better. He'd had a lot of friends who'd wanted to get to know her. They'd either fluttered around Julie or fluttered around her dad. And then they were gone. Like Stephen's birds. Lindsay didn't sound as though she fluttered. She sounded as though she glided.

"Whew, it's like a barn in here," said Dad, giving a big sniff. They were standing in front of the elephant, watching the keeper shovel hay into its cage.

"Remember," he said, "when we went to that farm, and you fed the baby lamb with a bottle?" He put his arm around her shoulder, but she pulled away from him and started over toward the giraffes. Of course she remembered and right now it made her feel bad to remember.

"I don't know who had more curls," said Dad, following her. "You or the baby lamb."

"Oh, Dad," said Julie. Sometimes he was so much fun and sometimes he was so insensitive.

"What's wrong?" he asked. It sounded as though he knew and didn't really want her to tell him. He didn't think ahead. That's what her mom used to complain. About how people would react.

"One more place before lunch," he said, looking at his watch. "Birds, monkeys, what'll it be?"

"Birds, I guess," said Julie. On such a gray day it would seem like a miracle to step through swinging strings of beads into the lush warmth of the tropical rain forest at the center of the bird house. It was an inside jungle with tall trees and vines, plants with thin, prickly leaves, and birds nesting at the tops of the trees. If there were a lot of people, the birds stayed high on the trees and on the artificial rock cliff. But if you were the only person and it was a quiet day and you were quiet, the birds came down from the heights, hopping around you and landing on branches right by your shoulder.

"Let's jog," said her dad when they got outside. "Like elephants." He ran off swinging an imaginary trunk. Julie followed reluctantly, thinking that she didn't need to meet Lindsay to know how much she hated her. Suppose she let her father go on without her, loping along in that comical way until he bumped into Lindsay. "Here's my daughter, Julie," he'd say. And he'd discover she wasn't there and then he'd feel guilty, because he would know she ran away because she didn't want to meet Lindsay.

"You're a pretty lazy elephant," Dad called back to her. He was still swinging his arms. It was hard to upset him for long and his buoyant good humor was irresistible. Julie walked faster and then ran to catch up with him.

"Why, here's my favorite elephant," said her father as she came alongside him and they started jogging in rhythm. It was hard to stay angry and jog, because jogging required all your energy. And it was impossible to stay cold. When they rounded the cage with long-legged wading birds standing on one foot, as though it was too cold to put down both feet, and started up the hill past the birds of prey, Julie took off her mittens and unzipped her jacket halfway. They were too breathless to talk. Julie didn't want to anyhow. But jogging together, straining on together eased the tension between them. It was probably Lindsay's idea. Still, he shouldn't have let her come. This time the judgment came to Julie in a passionless form.

But later, inside the bird house, the resentment against her father, Lindsay, she wasn't sure whom, welled up again. It seemed as though she had just sat down on the low, stone wall in the tropical rain forest. She had just started to savor spring in the midst of winter (the cawing and squawking of birds, the warm, earthy smells) when her father started looking at his watch. She ignored him and concentrated on sitting still enough to look like a part of the wall so that the timid birds would hop nearer. A blue-and-green bird with an elegant, trailing tail, pecking its way through the bushes, saw her and fluttered up to the treetops. I don't blame you, she thought. You've got to be careful of people, or they'll hurt you.

Dad sat down next to her as though they had plenty of time. But there he was looking at his watch again. For someone who was always late, he was certainly worrying a lot about the time. Finally, he leaned over and whispered tentatively, "I could go meet Lindsay and come back. I don't know how it got so late."

"I'll come." Julie didn't say it very graciously. She didn't want to be hurried, but she didn't want to be somewhere, alone, waiting for a second time that day.

At the door, Julie zipped up her jacket and started to put on her mittens. But she only had one. One of the two red mittens that her grandmother in Boston had knitted for her.

"Oh, dear," Julie said.

"What is it?" her dad asked.

"Nothing," said Julie. When you're angry at some-one, it's hard to admit that you've made a mistake, like losing a mitten.

As they walked along quickly, Julie felt in her pockets. A dollar bill on one side. But no mitten. The fare card on the other. But no mitten. Darn it! She felt awful about losing it. Because it was a present from her grandmother and matched her hat and scarf. And because now she'd have one cold hand.

"Want to jog again?" her dad asked.

"Okay," said Julie. It would be a way of keeping the one hand warm. Lost-a-mit-ten, lost-a-mit-ten, lost-for-ev-er-one-red-mit-ten. The words marched themselves unbidden through Julie's brain as she jogged along. While they were retracing their steps, Julie looked on the ground unavailingly for the mitten. There were piles of dirty snow, tufts of grass, a few candy wrappers, but no red mitten.

Then they diverged from the path to the elephant house and turned down into the park. Julie didn't want to ask her dad to take the time to retrace their steps further. Not when he was in such an obvious hurry. As the descent got steeper, their jogging got faster until it became running. Lostamitten, lostamitten, lost-foreveroneredmitten. The words were marching again, double time.

"Here we are," said her dad, stopping. "Or are we?" he panted. He sounded as breathless as Julie felt.

"There's a sign," said Julie, "on the pole by the steps." Her dad hurried over to read it.

"Bears that-a-way," said her dad. "Follow me."

Up the stairs, to the bears. New words capered into her brain. Julie felt dizzy from running and breathing in so much oxygen.

Her dad hurried on ahead past the row of bear cages, muttering the names to himself and looking.

"She's not here," he said, coming back toward Julie.

"Maybe she's late," said Julie. He ought to know how that was.

"That's not it," he said. "She's not here and the polar bears aren't here."

"They're probably in their caves." Julie couldn't see why he was so upset.

"No, their names aren't here!"

"Are you sure?" Julie followed him back, reading the names of the bears. Brown Bear, Grizzly Bear, Asian Black Bear. "That was where they used to be, wasn't it?" Julie said. And finally, Smokey the Bear.

What a dilemma! Dad was walking up and down, checking the signs a third time. "Maybe she's been already, and left because we weren't here and there weren't any polar bears," he fretted.

Even though she was angry at him, Julie felt sorry for him. It was upsetting to think of someone waiting the way she had, in the cold, making a special effort to come, and then being disappointed and going away.

"There must be polar bears somewhere," she said. "The zoo's always had them. Let's look for a map." They were near the center of the zoo now, where the restaurant and bathrooms were. Julie thought she remembered a map near the telephones. Telephones!

"Oh," she said, "I forgot to call Mom. And she'll be worrying."

"What a mess," said her father. "Call her right away. I'll look for a map."

Julie took her mitten off to put the money in the phone and held the receiver in her unmittened hand. My, it was cold! Each number she pushed felt like an ice cube. She listened to the phone ring—three times, four times. Suppose Mom wasn't there. Suppose Mom had gone out looking for her. On the fifth ring, Stephen answered.

"Oh, Julie," he said, "your mom'll be glad to hear from you." Julie thought he sounded disapproving.

"Hello, dear. Everything all right?"

"Mom, I'm sorry. I forgot. And we just got to a phone anyhow."

"That's what I imagined," said her mother.

"Julie," her father was at her elbow, "I found them."

"Mom, I've got to go," said Julie, hanging up.

"You follow the blue footprints. They start down there. See. Blue polar-bear prints. That's named the polar-bear trail."

The trail curved around behind the restaurant. Julie knew that eventually it led to the seals and sea lions.

"I hope she waited," said Dad, slowing down to look at his watch. "One-twenty, that's not too bad."

At the bottom of the cliff, below where they had been standing in front of the bear cages a few minutes ago, was a whole new creation—an enormous cage, with bright, new simulated rock and a green oval pool. Sitting at the edge, gazing enthusiastically at his or her reflection, was a big, white polar bear.

"When did they do that?" said her father. "Why

didn't they tell me? But we've probably missed her. She's probably come and given up."

And I should feel glad, thought Julie, but she didn't. After all, nothing from here on would be much fun if Dad had to worry about Lindsay.

"Do you think she might have made the same mistake?" asked Julie.

"That's it," he said. "That's where she is. I told her right next to Smokey the Bear. Come on, Julie. Oh I'm sorry, darling. You must be very tired. If you weren't all grown up, I'd carry you."

There! Dad was such a sweetheart. And he looked so flustered. And how could she help but love him, no matter what.

"Maybe I should stay here, Dad," she suggested, "in case Lindsay,"—it made her feel strange to say the name, to evoke that person she'd never seen—"Lindsay," she said, "came here while we're going there."

"You're a genius," said her dad. "If she comes, tell her I'll be right back."

"But, Dad . . . ." He was halfway up the path behind the restaurant already. So Julie asked herself, "What does she look like?" She put her unmittened hand in her pocket and asked the polar bear, "What does Lindsay look like?" The polar bear was too preoccupied with the misty image of itself to respond.

"Tall, wouldn't you say?" Julie ignored the polar bear's lack of interest. "With hair drawn severely back in a tortoise-shell clip. Wearing a tailored gray suit with black-patent-leather walking shoes. A mink jacket?" Julie thought she felt a drop of rain. What was she supposed to do? Stand there and get drenched waiting for her father's girl friend. The polar bear was pacing up and down, pausing now and then to put a paw in the water as though to test the temperature.

"Great day for a swim," said Julie.

"Isn't it though?" said a voice bright as a sunbeam. Not next to her, but further down, someone else was leaning on the rail watching the polar bear. Someone who had landed as lightly as a bird. Julie had never heard her come. And she looked like one too. Like a tropical bird escaped from the tropical rain forest.

She was wearing a woven cloak, something South American looking, yellow with a green border. And she had on an orange scarf, orange mittens and soft, tan, suede boots. That's why she had come so quietly. A mass of frizzy curls flared out around her head and hung down her back *and* she had big, golden loops hanging through her ears. She couldn't be. . . . "You aren't . . . ." She was only a girl. Not much taller than Julie. And not old enough to be her father's friend.

"I'm not what?" said the girl. She wasn't pretty, but her voice made you think she was. It seemed to mean so much to her father that Julie thought she'd better ask.

"You aren't Lindsay?" said Julie.

"That's me," said the girl. "Then you're Julie," she said.

"Yes," said Julie. "Did you go to the other place?" "Where?"

"Where the other bears are. My dad's there looking for you. He was afraid you'd given up."

"No, I'm just late," said Lindsay. "I always am. Your dad should have guessed. Look! The bear's going in."

Lindsay moved closer to Julie and pointed as the big, white bear shambled into the water. It swam on top with its head sticking out and its ears back like a dog. Then it dove under for a minute and came up to the top at the other end of the pool.

"I'll bet we can go down and watch it." Lindsay pointed to some steps at the side of the cage. "And when your dad comes, we'll pop out and surprise him."

"Okay," said Julie. "And if it rains, we'll be dry there."

The steps led down to a narrow tunnel that ran the length of the pool with steps going up and out at the other end. One could actually come in either way. One side of the tunnel was a concrete wall and the other side was a huge picture window with a view of cloudy green water.

"Where's the bear?" said Lindsay. "Has it stopped swimming already? It needs more exercise."

"There it is," said Julie. "It's coming our way."

Out of the green murk a big, white body swooshed toward them, executing a graceful turn as it passed. Its white fur glistened silver in the light that filtered down through the water.

"Oh," said Lindsay, "that's the most wonderful thing I've ever seen."

"Yes," said Julie. "We're close enough to touch it, if the glass wasn't there."

"And the fur would feel like silk," said Lindsay. They stayed watching, silent, while the bear came around again and again. Mindlessly, rhythmically, up and down it circled the pool.

"Julie!"

"It's my dad calling," said Julie.

"I know," said Lindsay. "Let's tiptoe up the steps and surprise him."

"No, I'll go," said Julie, "and pretend you haven't gotten here."

"Great," said Lindsay. "Then I'll pop out behind you."

"Okay," said Julie. They started up the stairs, holding in their giggles as they went.

"Grrrr!"

"Help!"

"Ooooh!" Julie screamed.

"Got you both," said Dad. He must have come down the other stairs and crept along the tunnel behind them.

"You sneak," said Lindsay.

"And what were you doing?" said Dad.

"Now that Lindsay's here"—Julie said her name as though she'd known it for years—"do you think we could eat?"

They ordered hot dogs and french fries. Junk food, Mom would have said. Hot chocolate for Julie and coffee for Dad and Lindsay. When Lindsay was with Dad, she did things that made her seem older, like letting him help her off with her cloak and drinking coffee.

They had their choice of booths in the restaurant. Julie noticed a man and a little boy who were sitting at a table near them and looked as though they didn't know what to say to each other. Divorced, thought Julie. She wondered whether people could tell about them. Certainly not because they were quiet, because

Lindsay always had something to say. She told them about forgetting that she had left her clothes in the basement dryer of her apartment building so she had to run back from the bus stop to get them. Which meant she missed her bus. Which meant she was late, but *fortunately* Julie was there.

"How's school?" she asked Julie between sips of coffee. "This is hot," she said. "Your dad told me you just changed schools." That was the question Dad was supposed to ask and then Julie was supposed to ask about having help with math. But now, as usual, was not the time.

"My dad worked for IBM," said Lindsay. "Which really means, I've Been Moved. I went to four schools in four years and I read *Julius Caesar* four times."

"I guess you knew it by heart," Julie's dad said.

"That was the worst of it," said Lindsay. "I couldn't remember between times. Not to identify quotes and that sort of thing."

"What about math?" said Julie. She was really skating close to the edge.

"A disaster," said Lindsay. "Every school was doing something different and doing it a different way. I was always being tutored."

"That's why you're an accountant," said Dad.

"Yes, that's probably why," agreed Lindsay. "All that attention probably helped me to understand math better than most of the other kids. But at the time I was really embarrassed. I was sure everyone thought I was the dumbest kid in the school."

"That's how I'd feel," said Julie. She was sure she had given herself away.

"One gets over it, though. A couple years later, who

cares?" said Lindsay. "Besides, one year I had this cute boy helping me."

"I can imagine," said Julie's father.

Julie thought of Arnold Finch.

"He'd walk me home after school. And we'd drink Cokes and discuss math. Pretty romantic." Julie wished that Cal could tutor her in math instead of Arnold Finch.

"I'll bet Julie's found someone she likes," said Lindsay. "Boys? Girls? Teachers? I'll bet you've met someone nice already."

"Oh, I have," said Julie. If Dad hadn't been there, she would have told Lindsay all about Cal and Cynthia and Rosalie and Mrs. Mitchell and the stray cat. Even about Mr. Hawkins and the C-minus. Maybe she could tell Lindsay about Stephen. Talking would make her feel less boxed in. Julie yearned for the release of talking to someone about everything.

"Better be moving on," said Dad, standing up. "It's TV time for the gorillas."

"It's apartment cleaning time for me," said Lindsay, reaching for her yellow cloak. "There're cat hairs all over everything."

"You should see Lindsay's cat," Dad said. "It's Tibetan."

"Almost. Himalayan." Lindsay laughed. "Give the gorillas my love." As Dad helped to arrange Lindsay's cloak, Julie saw his hand linger on her shoulder in an intimate, proprietary way. "Two's company." I always seem to be the extra person, Julie thought. Who do I have who's just mine, special for me alone? she wondered.

Julie put on her jacket and her one mitten. And I've

lost my favorite red mitten, she thought gloomily.

"You dropped a mitten, Julie." Lindsay's voice was like a caress. "Is it under your chair?" Lindsay was looking on the floor.

"It's not here," said Julie. "I lost it earlier."

"Any idea where?" said her father.

"I'm always losing things," said Lindsay, "so I'm very good at finding them. Where do you last remember having both mittens?" she demanded.

"In the elephant house," said Julie. She hated to bother Dad and Lindsay. But she did want her special red mitten back.

"And where were you when you found that it was missing?"

"The Case of the Missing Mitten," said Dad.

"At the bird house," said Julie.

"Aha!" said Lindsay. "We'll form a search party."

"Where shall we start, Holmes?" said Dad.

"What do you say, Watson?" asked Lindsay, turning to Julie. One minute Dad and Lindsay seemed separate and grown-up and the next they seemed younger and sillier than Julie.

"I guess the bird house," said Julie.

They retraced their steps up the hill to the bird house, walking more slowly as they got close. No mitten.

"It's not worth the trouble," said Julie.

"Yes, it is," said Lindsay. "Lost things are always somewhere."

They came back down the hill past the birds of prey and around the cage with the wading birds.

"I remember," said Julie, "I took my mittens off on the other side as we were jogging."

"So that, Dr. Watson, is where I predict the missing mitten—"

"Unless someone picked it up," said Julie.

"Or it's escaped," said Dad. "Hurry, there's no time to be lost!" They ran around to the other side of the cage.

"I see it!" said Lindsay.

"So do I," said Julie.

"Don't let it get away," said Dad.

Julie picked it up with her mittened hand and gave it to her unmittened hand. It was like finding a long lost friend. "Thanks, Lindsay," said Julie, slipping it on. Mittens were much warmer than pockets. "Lucky you were here." She never thought she'd be saying that!

Lindsay went to the great apes house with them after all. Julie's father said they would give her a lift back on the way home.

"I shouldn't," she insisted. "I should be vacuuming."

"Oh, stay a little longer," Julie found herself urging. She'd have a chance to ask her father about math after they dropped Lindsay off, and she could tell he wanted Lindsay to stay.

When they left the great apes house, it had really started to rain—a cold rain that might as well have been snow.

"Had enough?" said Dad.

"For sure," said Julie. "If you . . . ." She turned to Lindsay.

"I should have been vacuuming an hour ago," said Lindsay.

They all sat in the front seat of Dad's car. "You

first," said Lindsay as they were getting in. They drove back up Connecticut Avenue several blocks past the Van Ness metro stop and turned into a circular driveway in front of a tall, old, brick apartment building with a string of bay windows reaching high above the tops of the trees.

"That's where I live," said her father. "Eighth floor."

"Whereas I'm only a third-floor peasant," Lindsay added. "See you." She closed the car door, flapped her yellow cloak in farewell, and ran up the steps to the apartment building.

"Now I think I'd better take you right home," said her father, "before this freezes. By next time my apartment'll be fixed up for entertaining."

"That's okay," said Julie. She was ready to go home. All the walking and jogging and fresh air had made her sleepy. She wanted to snuggle down under her quilt and read and fall asleep.

"Dad, I've been meaning to ask," she said as they drove through Rock Creek Park, which meant they were about a third of the way home. "I need some help with my math. It's like what Lindsay said, being in a new school and having different work." She was glad Lindsay had been there to prepare the way. "And I wondered if you could help me."

"Sure, monkey," said her father. "Bring your book along next time and we'll see if we can figure it out. We'll get Lindsay to help."

"Next weekend?" said Julie.

"Oh, I'd say in about three weeks. I'm going to be out of town at meetings for a week. I'll give you a call when I get back."

In that moment, Julie perceived the absurdity of the plan. Dad wasn't five blocks away anymore. He was half an hour by car and longer by metro. And he was going to be out of town for a week anyhow. She looked at the granite boulders littering the narrow stream that wound through the park parallel to the road. Had they been there during the Civil War, during the Revolutionary War? Lindsay was right. In a few years, maybe months, it wouldn't matter about math. It had already begun to hurt less. Julie was glad Mrs. Barker had arranged for her to start on Monday. Now it seemed like the easiest solution.

"I'll miss you," said her father as Julie got out of the car. "Once I get settled, you'll have to come for a long stay."

Suppose, thought Julie as she went up the steps and up the front walk of her house like a stranger coming for a visit, I lived with Dad, instead of Mom and Stephen. Would I feel less like a nuisance, even with Lindsay around? Her mother came to the door and opened it for her. And Julie's father waved and pulled away.

"Hello, sweetheart," said her mother, holding the door for her. "Did you have a good time? It's so nice to have you back."

But how could I ever leave Mom? Julie thought as she hung up her jacket and put her red scarf and her two red mittens in the hall bureau. And the ache of being pulled apart—one way by her love for her mother and the other by her love for her father—reminded Julie once again of her helplessness.

No Cake for Cats

"Well, I'd like to know who's going to work on the dance, then," said Rosalie. Julie had hoped that the freezing rain on Saturday would turn into snow on Sunday so that Monday would be a snow day, delaying the beginning of her tutoring sessions with Arnold Finch. Instead, the rain washed away the last piles of snow, and the starry sky on Sunday night promised a clear school day on Monday. And there they were, Julie and Cynthia and Rosalie, walking to school on Monday morning without even needing boots.

The stray cat followed them down the path. "Go home," said Julie when they got to East-West Highway. If the cat followed them across with the special policewoman who directed school traffic, it might try to get back when no one was there to stop the cars. "Go home, shoo," Julie insisted, waving her arms and imitating Stephen's emphatic inflection. Julie thought the cat looked surprised as it turned and scurried back down the path.

Cynthia and Rosalie had already crossed the street, but the traffic lady was still holding up her arms, so Julie ran after them.

"Sorry, but I'm tied up sixth period," said Cynthia. "Every day this week, except P.E. days."

"Don't tell me you're working on the school newspaper? I thought you didn't like to write."

What'll I say if she asks me? wondered Julie. That I have a date with Arnold Finch?

"It's a special activity that I'm not going to tell you about," said Cynthia.

"What's his name?" said Rosalie.

"Guess," said Cynthia.

"Oh, I'll find out soon enough. What about you?" Rosalie, who was walking a little bit behind, poked her head in between Cynthia and Julie.

"I'm busy too," said Julie.

"Another special activity?" asked Rosalie.

"Sort of," said Julie.

"Dances. Everybody wants them and nobody wants to do the work."

"But, Rosalie, I'd much rather . . . ." Julie didn't finish her sentence. Keeping a secret meant being careful of every little thing you said.

"If you met after school," suggested Cynthia.

"Next week. Every day," said Rosalie. "You've both got to promise to come," said Rosalie as they went in the door to the school.

"I do," said Cynthia. "I swear. Put me on the refreshment committee." The first bell rang before Julie had a chance to answer. She hadn't decided yet about whether she wanted to go to the dance. It wasn't at the top on her list of worries. At the top on her list of worries was getting tutored in math by Arnold Finch without anyone knowing. Sixth period in the conference room. Maybe she should wear a wig. She sat in history class, fifth period, wondering what color she would choose. Blond, like Cynthia's? Many of the heroines in *True Romance* had auburn hair. Wavy auburn hair. She thought she'd start with that.

"And the test will be on Monday," said Mrs. All-bright. "On chapters ten and eleven." A test on Monday! There was a groan as people slammed books shut.

"At least it's not the Monday after the dance," said Rosalie as they left. History was the only class they had together. "I've got to rush," she said. "Sure you can't come?"

Julie waited until Rosalie disappeared down the stairs at the far end of the hall. Then she checked all around her to see if there was anyone she knew, even Cal, which was unlikely since he was still invisible at school. Quickly she opened the door to the conference room. She was glad it was always kept closed and had an opaque curtain over the window. She expected the room to be empty. She hadn't seen Arnold go in. But two girls were sitting at the table. One she recognized from her English class. She was named Wilma and was very quiet. The other had her back to Julie. But the long, straight blond hair was familiar enough. It was Cynthia! Then Cynthia would know. And she'd tell Rosalie. All was lost. Except . . . .

"Hi," said Julie warily.

"Hi," said Wilma and looked down at her notebook.

"Why, hi, honey," said Cynthia. "You looking for somebody?"

"Arnold Finch." That didn't have to mean she was going to be tutored.

"Why, you aren't here for . . . ?" said Cynthia.

"You too?" said Julie. Cynthia nodded. "Do you have Mr. Hawkins?" Julie asked.

"Other section," said Cynthia. That was the end of her secret. A secret that two people knew didn't last. But it was the end of Cynthia's too.

"Are you just starting?" she asked Cynthia.

"Sit down, honey." Cynthia pulled out the chair next to her. "This is my first time alone with the super-brain. I don't think I need protection, but I'm glad you're here. Are you a math moron too?"

"In a way," said Julie. But she wasn't really. And she was glad of that.

"Good afternoon, girls," said Arnold Finch, stepping into the room with the poise and authority of a grown-up teacher. Julie couldn't believe he was the same boy who threw the snowball and whispered indictments of Mr. Hawkins in her ear.

"I think we'll go back to the beginning," he said, sitting down at the table across from them.

"Good," said Cynthia. "I didn't understand any of it."

"How about you?" he asked Wilma.

"What?" she said. She looked as though she was always afraid of giving the wrong answer. "Starting at the beginning," Arnold explained.

"Yes?" She said it like a question.

"Fine. And you?" he said, turning to Julie. When she looked at him, it was hard to take him seriously. He had pimples and his hair was stringy and too long. But he sounded as though he knew what he was doing.

"It's all new for me," said Julie, "except what I learned this month. Because of changing schools." She hoped no one would ask her why she had changed. Of course there were lots of other kids in her situation (maybe Wilma, maybe Arnold Finch). Still, being a child of divorced parents made her feel like a curiosity—something one wrote articles about after observing its habits, as one would study an animal in the zoo.

"Let's go over the first chapter and work out some of the problems," said Arnold.

By the time the bell rang, Julie felt she understood the first chapter fairly well. Cynthia seemed to be learning the material too, although Julie usually had the answers ready first. It was hard to tell about Wilma, because she said so little.

"That kid should quit being a student. He'd make a better teacher any day," said Cynthia as they left at the end of the period a few minutes after Arnold. He had assigned them problems to do for next time. "We can work on math together," said Cynthia. They forced a path through the crowded hall to their lockers.

"What about Rosalie?" asked Julie.

"Oh, I'll tell her sometime," Cynthia said. "Then everyone'll know, but boys like dumb girls better than bright ones."

Julie didn't care whether boys like dumb girls or bright girls. She only cared about what Cal liked. Was he all right? She hadn't seen him since the bike accident. She'd been away Saturday and it had rained on Sunday. If she hurried after school, she might get to him while he was still sorting newspapers.

"Meet you outside," Rosalie called as she passed. "I want to put my notes about the dance in my locker. We've got the committees all set up."

Julie couldn't tell Cynthia and Rosalie she didn't want to walk back with them, but she'd rather see Cal alone. He clearly didn't want to talk with Cynthia and

Rosalie. In fact, he seemed to be one of those boys who was uncomfortable with girls. Except with her, or except on snow days.

"There's a rumor, you two, that you were in the conference room with Arnold Finch," said Rosalie, the moment the three of them started walking. "What's up?" That was how long it took for everyone in the school to know what was going on—about fifteen minutes.

"Guess," said Cynthia. "But don't strain your little ole brain."

"He's helping you with math," said Rosalie. "You never would tell me what you got on your report."

Listening to Cynthia and Rosalie, Julie decided it was a waste of time to worry so much about a bad grade in math, especially when you couldn't prevent it. Of course, company made it less painful. She felt like running and laughing and throwing her books in the air. She'd tell Cal all about it when she saw him. He'd appreciate the joke—how she tried to be so secret. And then how she found Cynthia already sitting in the conference room.

Cal! She could glimpse him getting onto his bicycle as they turned down Raymond Street. There was no way she could catch up with him. And he wasn't going to slip and fall again, not with the snow all gone. Cal! There was no point in calling out to the figure that was spinning out of sight in the opposite direction.

The same thing happened every afternoon that week, like the rerun of an old TV show. First she would look down the street toward Cal's house and see him leave on his bicycle. Then Rosalie would say,

"See you tomorrow," and turn back toward her house. Cynthia and Julie would continue on down to Julie's, where they stood for a minute. Julie would wave to Captain Crunch, who was about to go inside. Finally, the cat, who had been nosing around Captain Crunch, would hasten across the street to welcome Cynthia and Julie.

"What a friendly, little ole pussy," Cynthia would say, stroking its back.

"I wish it was mine," Julie would say.

"Wanta come over and do math?"

"Sure!" Julie never liked going into an empty house. And each day she hoped that when she came back from Cynthia's she'd catch Cal returning on his bicycle. But each time there was nobody around—only the cat.

"You poor thing." Julie would stand very still while the cat rubbed against her. "Is anybody feeding you? No!" she'd say, when it would start to follow her up the driveway. "Cats aren't welcome here."

The cat would sit back and look up at her. Why? it would seem to ask.

"It's Stephen," she'd say. "He's not bad," she'd explain. "But he likes birds. And my mom," she'd add. And again she'd recognize a special affinity between herself and the stray cat.

As she lay in bed Saturday morning, enjoying the leisure of sleeping late, Julie resolved that before the day was over she would manage to talk with Cal. Let's see—she made a mental list. The bike accident and tutoring in math and also her conversation with Mrs. Mitchell. There was a lot to catch up on, and she suspected that if he had a chance to talk with her alone, Cal would stop being invisible.

All day she kept looking out of the window toward Cal's house. At noon, she went out and mailed a letter. After lunch she walked down to the corner grocery for milk. But she didn't see Cal. As she was coming back with the milk, it started to drizzle. By newspaper delivery time, it was raining hard. How would Cal manage? Maybe his father drove him around his route. There were no cars in the driveway.

Mom and Stephen urged her to go out for dinner with them, but Julie refused. She was tired of being the third person with her mother and Stephen, or with her father and Lindsay.

"We'll go to Swensens for ice cream," her mother coaxed.

"I have homework," said Julie. "A history test on Monday." It was hard to argue with that excuse. "And maybe I'll make a chocolate cake and invite someone over to eat it with me."

"What a good idea," said her mother. "Why don't you call now and get it arranged."

"Don't worry, Mom. I'll do it later, if I do." Mom seemed overanxious. It made Julie wish she hadn't made the suggestion at all.

Stephen came into the kitchen while she was beating the cake batter. He hung his dripping coat on the kitchen door. He'd been out filling the bird feeder.

"You should join us," he shouted over the electric beater. The afternoon was such a depressing one that Julie was tempted to change her mind. If Stephen hadn't been standing with his back to her, looking out, of course, at the bird feeder, she probably would have. But she wasn't sure he really wanted her. Why should he? People who were in love wanted to be alone together.

After the cake had cooled, Julie started to ice it. Chocolate cake with chocolate icing. It was almost dinnertime—dark and still raining. Mom stood at the kitchen door, buttoning her lacy cuffs. She was wearing the gold bangles that Stephen had given her for Christmas.

"Why don't you come after all?" she suggested. "I hate to leave you here alone on such a dreary night."

"No, thanks," said Julie. She didn't know why she resisted their kindly urgings. Especially when she already felt lonely, even before they'd left. Did she still hope for word from Cal? Or did she imagine she would telephone him? Girls did call boys. But Julie doubted whether she was bold enough.

"Be sure to keep the door locked," her mother said as Stephen held her coat for her.

Wait! I've changed my mind, Julie wanted to say. But it was too late.

"You needn't be afraid," said Stephen. "After living here for three years, I know it's a safe neighborhood."

"Good-bye, dear." Mom kissed her on the cheek and then went out the door with Stephen following.

Julie waited in the kitchen while they left. She could see her mother turning to wave good-bye before she went out the porch door. Julie stood there another minute thinking she should heat the oven and get her TV dinner started. Was that a noise she heard in the living room, a kind of tapping? Julie knew that one always heard noises, imaginary noises, when one was alone in a house.

I'll turn on the light, she decided. That'll make me feel safer. But her mother already had the corner lamp on. Maybe the noise came from upstairs. She stood still again in the living room and listened. Did she hear it? Tap. Tap.

"All right," Julie said to herself. "Go upstairs. You know it's nothing. But you'll feel better with lights on up there too." She stood at the foot of the stairs, looking up into the darkness. Did she hear the noise? No, of course not. She walked upstairs defiantly and turned on the light in the hall and then a light in the guest room, because it seemed the most empty.

What about the bathroom? Did she hear the noise again? Was it downstairs? Was the back door locked? She couldn't really remember. She hadn't checked to see. She had assumed that Stephen . . . . Get it locked before anyone snuck in. Hurry! Down the stairs. No one in the hall. No one in the kitchen. And the door was locked. Of course it was. Whereas Dad always left doors unlocked, Stephen always left them locked.

In the bright warmth of the kitchen with a delicious chocolate cake waiting to be eaten, Julie decided to put her TV dinner in the oven and stop worrying about noises. Stephen had said it was a safe neighborhood. And who wanted to be out breaking into houses on a cold, wet night? After dinner she'd call somebody, Cynthia or Rosalie. Or even Wendy. If she'd been at home alone in the apartment in Virginia, Wendy would have been right down the hall, a minute away from popping over.

By the time she was savoring the last bits of enchillada and refried beans and watching "Once Upon a Classic" on TV Julie felt much calmer. She was too interested in the program to listen for noises. It was a dramatization of *The Secret Garden,* a story she knew so well she felt she had lived it herself.

Dickon made her think of Cal with his teasing, friendly manner. Maybe he'd find a way to take care of the stray cat, Julie thought. The way Dickon made pets out of the wild creatures on the moors.

Being alone isn't so bad, Julie thought as she switched off the TV. Doing what I want when I want to do it. There was no reason to be scared. She knew that Cal was across the street and Mrs. Mitchell . . . . It was doubtful whether she'd ask Mrs. Mitchell for help in an emergency. "I'll have some chocolate cake now," she said to herself. "And then I'll call somebody. And then I'll have some more."

As she was cutting her first piece of cake, she was startled by a loud banging on the back porch. There was nothing uncertain about this noise. Its reality is undeniable. This is it, she thought. All evening I've known it was coming. There was something relaxing about the certainty that IT had finally arrived.

With her hand still holding the knife in the cake, she looked over at the door, in case it had gotten unlocked. Which was, of course, impossible. And the light was on, stupid. There was no one out there. She could see that clearly enough. A pause, and then another bang. What to do? A robber wouldn't make all that noise, she reflected. Her hold on the knife loosened a bit. But what could it be? Nothing to be seen from where she was standing. Julie put down the knife and tiptoed over. Whoever it was, whatever it was, she wanted to catch it. With her hand on the doorknob, she looked out. No, still nothing there. The porch seemed empty. But it was a real noise. Had it been the wind blowing the door? She looked down at the floor. "Oh!" she cried out. "Oh!" Poised for a leap up to the doorknob of the porch door was a gray-striped, tabby cat with white paws.

"You," said Julie to the cat. "You! You scared me half to death."

"*Meow,*" said the cat.

"What were you doing?" said Julie. How was it possible for a cat to make so much noise? She looked down questioningly as it stood staring back up at her.

"*Meow,*" it said again.

"What are you trying to tell me, pussy?" Julie cautiously opened the door, then stepped onto the cold, damp porch, closing the door behind her. The porch screen door was slightly open and banged gently as the wind blew it.

"Is that why you were making all that noise?" Julie said to the cat. "Were you trying to open the door? What a clever cat you are," she said as the cat rubbed its head affectionately against her legs. "Did you want to get out?" she asked. When she opened the porch door, the rain blew in against her face.

"No, you don't want to go out there." But it couldn't stay. Not until Stephen got home. "And I wouldn't be allowed to keep you, but I wish I would," she said to the cat. She stood for a moment holding the door open, looking out at the wet bricks of the patio shining in the rain.

"You don't want to go, do you?" Julie repeated. The cat continued to nuzzle her. She closed the door and knelt down to stroke it. "What am I going to do with you, cat? I can't force you out on a night like this." The cat stretched out on the porch carpeting and started to purr. "Look here, kitty," Julie said. "Don't get so contented. I can't stay here with you any longer. It's too cold. And I can't let you in the house. Although I don't know why not. There aren't any birds inside for you to eat."

"*R-r-r-r.*" said the cat. Julie could feel the purring vibrating under the cat's chin.

"Maybe you could spend one night on the porch," said Julie. "You couldn't hurt anything by doing that. Look, kitty, I've got to go in. It's so cold. And I'll have to think about what to do. Oh, I wish I didn't have to leave you." She stood up and put her hand on the kitchen doorknob. The cat stood up too and came over by the door.

"No," said Julie. "No, you'll have to wait." She pushed the cat aside with her foot, opened the door, slipped inside, and banged the door shut. Oh, I hope I haven't hurt it, Julie thought. She looked out of the window again. The cat was trying to nudge the porch door open with its nose. I should have locked it, Julie thought, then it couldn't leave. But it wouldn't be dumb enough to leave in all this rain, she reassured herself. Was there someone else who would keep the cat for the night? Not Cal, since Captain Crunch was allergic to cats. She'd have her piece of cake and then call Cynthia. But as she sat down to eat a big piece of chocolate cake with chocolate icing, she heard "*meow.*" "At least the cat's still there," she said to herself and took the first, luscious bite of cake.

"*Meow,*" she heard again.

"Oh, kitty, be quiet," she said and took a second bite.

"Meow," the cat continued. It sounded plaintive, urgent, like a baby crying.

"What am I going to do?" Julie said to herself. She couldn't go on eating chocolate cake with the cat sounding miserable on the back porch. Once more she got up and looked out the back door. There was no cat in sight.

"But I just heard it," she said to herself. "Is it gone?" And she opened the door to see. Instantly, a gray-striped tabby cat flashed past her into the kitchen.

"Wait," she cried and ran to close the door into the hall. Then she went back and closed the outside door. The cat was sitting back on its haunches, looking around the kitchen and twitching its tail.

"I guess you're pleased with yourself," said Julie. She sat down cross-legged on the floor next to it. "Well, it's not my fault." The cat looked at her. "You don't care," said Julie, "but Mom and Stephen will. Stephen especially will." The cat put its paws up on her knee and crawled into her lap. It stretched and then curled up comfortably in the little hollow Julie's crossed legs made.

"Nice kitty," said Julie. Underneath the soft fur, she could feel the warm, breathing companionship of the cat. A few minutes of stroking in the heated kitchen seemed to put the cat to sleep.

Now what am I going to do? Julie wondered. She looked around the kitchen from her vantage point on the floor. Oh, yes, she thought when she saw a plate on the table with a piece of chocolate cake on it, that's what I was doing.

"If I really stretch," she said to herself, looking down to see if she was disturbing the cat, "very carefully, I can just about reach . . . ." She was able to get the edge of the plate with her thumb and forefinger and pull it across the table to where she could pick it up.

"Yum," she said a few minutes later as she scraped up the icing and the last crumbs. "Do you like chocolate cake, kitty?" she asked the cat. Its eyes were closed. In and out. She could feel its deep, regular breathing expand and contract against her legs.

"You're not worrying," she said to the cat, "but I am." She put the cake plate back on the table. "What am I going to do with you now?" she asked the cat. Here was a little life that had put its trust in her. It made her feel important and old in a worrisome way. She leaned back against the kitchen cabinets, careful not to dislocate the sleeping cat, and thought of possible plans. None of them seemed acceptable.

"It won't do to send you back into the rain," she said. "That's out. You could stay here until I go to bed, but then . . . ."

When her mom and Stephen came home, would they be more upset to find a cat in the kitchen or on the back porch? Julie speculated. If she left a note, what would she say? Mentally, she tried out a few phrases, none of which seemed to dispel the shock of coming back late at night to discover a strange cat just outside or just inside one's kitchen door. And they'd probably send it away, she decided. Unless I was here to plead for it. She could try to stay awake till then, but she already felt sleepy ("Just like you, kitty," she said) and they might go to a movie or shopping and it was only eight-thirty.

"It wouldn't be so bad, would it," she asked the cat, "if I took you up to my room?" The cat gave a big, approving yawn so that Julie could see its pink tongue and its sharp teeth. Much sharper than Mrs. Mitchell's, she thought. The cat stuck out its paws, front and back, as far as they would go, opened its eyes, crawled up onto her knee and jumped to the floor. After brushing a few cat hairs off of her jeans, Julie stood up. Ouch! She felt stiff from sitting cross-legged for so long.

"Then," said Julie to the cat, who was now exploring the kitchen, "tomorrow morning, before anyone else is up, I'll sneak you back outside. And you must never come back again. It's like coming to Bluebeard's Castle," she said as she cut herself another middle-sized piece of cake. "I'd give you some cake, but I don't think it's on your diet. Whatever your diet is. No cake for cats," she said.

By the time she had finished eating and had cleared up her supper dishes, the cat was sitting down licking itself. "What a contortionist you are," Julie said. "You can wash every part of yourself, except for your whiskers." How was she going to get this creature upstairs? Would it follow her without running off to another part of the house? That was unlikely. She contemplated the cat. "How do I pick you up?" she said to herself. She could call someone and ask. She had been planning to call, but now she didn't need anyone. Now that she had the cat for company.

Nuisance

"It can't be too difficult," she said to the cat as it squeezed between the legs of the kitchen chair and her legs. She'd seen Cal pick it up when they were shoveling Mrs. Mitchell's path. How? Hadn't he grabbed it by the middle? "Promise you won't bite or scratch," she told the cat.

"Come on, kitty," she said. The cat had chosen that moment to lie down under the kitchen table. Julie saw herself crawling under to catch it, while the cat walked out the other side. "I'm going to be clever," she warned the cat, moving toward the hall door as though she was going to open it. As she suspected, the cat, eager to explore, with one quick, silent motion was standing by the door ready to slip through the moment Julie opened it.

"You're a tricky one too, aren't you?" Julie said. "I'm not going to chase you all over the house." She bent down to pick the cat up by the middle. Being inexperienced, Julie was tentative. Would the cat mind? "Remember, no nonsense." It looked awkward to Julie, with lots of cat legs and tail hanging over the edges. "Sorry, I don't think I've got it quite right," Julie apologized. But the cat seemed unperturbed.

After managing to get the cat up to her room without dropping it, she dumped it on her couch and hurried back to close the door. She had not yet been able to turn on the light. For a moment, she waited in the dark. She could see the silhouette of the cat, its back arched with excitement, standing on the couch. The streetlight glinted through its eyes in a way that made them look strangely red and malevolent. The wind-blown raindrops studded the window with chips of light. Briefly, she wondered what strange, wild bit of nature she had welcomed into her room. Would the cat jump off the couch and attack her?

"Meow," said a mild, questioning little voice. Julie, as though released from a trance, switched on the light.

"Oh, kitty," she said, kneeling by the couch and stroking it. "Did you wonder too? Did you wonder whether you had come to the house of an evil witch?"

"Meow," said the cat again.

"You don't need to worry, kitty. There aren't any evil witches around here. Only a friendly one." The cat put its paws up on the windowsill as though it was trying to look out.

"No, that's not the witch's house," Julie explained. "That's the house where two brave princes live, Prince Cal and Prince Captain Crunch. You can't see the witch's house from here," she continued as the cat stretched out on the couch and started to purr. "But someday, I'll introduce you. Or maybe you should go over and introduce yourself. In case she needs a cat. Except I think she may have retired from riding broomsticks."

After changing to her nightgown, Julie made a fast exit to the bathroom. When she got back, the cat was still lying on the couch with its eyes closed. Julie was pleased to see it comfortably settled.

"You've made yourself at home," she said. A rainy gust of wind spattered against the window. "Imagine," she admonished the sleeping cat, "you might be out in that. I hope you appreciate what I've done for you. And," she added, "the risks I've taken for you."

Julie looked at the digital clock by her bed. It sat there like a parent, like a stepfather, slicing her life into little arbitrary pieces—9:37—pause—9:38—pause—9:39. Most of the stores closed at nine, but if they went to a movie, her mother and Stephen wouldn't be back until midnight.

Was the cat tired enough from its wanderings to sleep through the night? Should she wake it now and keep it awake until 11:30 so it would sleep more soundly later? But suppose they came home sooner? Besides, she didn't want to stay awake until 11:30.

Julie turned on her bed lamp and turned off the overhead light. She'd get into bed very quietly without disturbing the cat and read for a while before going to sleep. She opened the other window a crack and spread out her quilt. It was a special quilt, a lifetime quilt that her Boston grandmother had started for her when she was born. It was composed of squares with pictures made from colored material stitched on with small, almost invisible stitches. Her grandmother had made one every year since she was born and sewed it on over a blank, white square.

Each picture represented some event in her life, starting with the red-and-white ball she had when she was tiny. There was a picture of her teddy bear and a birthday cake with four candles and her two-wheeled bicycle. And there was a square with a picture of the sailboat they used to have, *The Turnabout.* Her mother hadn't liked the tippy feeling of being in a sailboat. And her father could spend the whole day out on the bay. All of that seemed so far away. Everything seemed to have "turned about."

"If you were my cat, I'd ask her to make a picture of you, kitty," Julie said. "I'm going to visit Grand- mother and take the quilt so she can teach me to sew on the squares. She said she would someday."

Julie ran her fingers over the pictures as she lay in bed. She could feel each of the four candles and the wheels on the bicycle. How good it was to be in bed with cool, fresh sheets and a warm quilt. She propped up the pillow behind her and looked over at the cat. It was still asleep, thank goodness. At least she didn't have to worry about it being out in the rain. Having a cat snoozing on her couch was almost as good as hav- ing a friend over to spend the night. Julie savored its companionship as she picked up her *True Romance* magazine and started to read. "A strange noise made him turn around and grab her hand." Julie forgot about everything else as she read on. "She'd never seen him look so serious. Not frightened, but strong and urgent."

Suddenly, the loud noise of a car door banging shut penetrated into the world of the story. They're back. Mom might come in to talk with me, she thought, and turned out the light. Then she closed the magazine, put it back on the table, and slid down under the covers. I'd better seem to be asleep, she thought. She lay listening for the sound of the back door opening and feeling guilty, as though she'd just told a lie.

"I haven't done anything wrong," she argued with

herself. "It's kindness to animals. Birds are used to managing in the rain, but cats . . . ."

She still hadn't heard the back door open. Maybe she was wrong. Maybe it had been the door of a car parked out in the street. But just in case, she continued to lie very still. It isn't Mom I'm worried about, she thought. She's never minded about cats one way or the other. It was only that we couldn't have pets in our apartment. But Stephen. How would he react to having a cat as an overnight guest? He was so emotional about cats.

She sat up in bed and listened carefully. No more noises. It must have been a false alarm. Even so, Julie didn't want to risk turning the light on again. She lay in the dark listening to the rain and the faint sound of the cat's breathing. It was so faint that— Julie sat up again and looked. Was the cat still there? She couldn't quite tell. Quietly, she crawled down to the bottom of her bed. From that point, she could see the cat, a black hump on the couch, dimly outlined by the light from the street.

She leaned back against the foot of the bed and looked out through the raindrops toward the street. Could she see anyone walking along or bicycling? Would Cal be coming back from a party? Did he go to parties? Had she ever seen him look "strong and urgent"? The eyes that teased her from behind his steel-rimmed glasses simply seemed friendly and interested. What would Cal think if he knew she had the stray cat in her room. "You're a brave princess, Jewel." She felt brave. It was like hiding a runaway slave.

Brrr! Time to get back under the covers. The rain droned on as Julie imagined herself telling Cal about the cat. What would happen to it next? How would the story end? Without expecting to, lulled by the sound of the rain, Julie fell asleep.

Or was she still awake? A baby was crying. Wailing pathetically. Where was it? She must help it. No, it wasn't a baby. It was a cat. *Meow, meow.* It was the stray cat in danger. She must help it. It was drowning. Julie was in her nightgown, running along the street through the rain. In the distance, she saw someone standing on Mrs. Mitchell's porch. Was it her father? Her *own* father? Holding something. Was it the cat? In his arms. *Meow, meow.*

Julie felt light footsteps across her back and sleepily heard something thud softly to the floor. Without really waking up, she told herself it was the cat. *Meow! Meow!* "Oh, be quiet!" she told the cat. Had she said it out loud, or not? It was so hard to wake up. She was still standing on the street looking toward the figure on Mrs. Mitchell's porch. *Meow. Meow.* Julie slipped away from dreams down to the silent, shrouded bottom of sleep.

"Help! Help! Stephen, help!" Mom was screaming. Julie sat up in bed. The light from the hall came in through the open door. Was anyone there? No. But Julie could hear Stephen calling.

"Marjorie, for heaven's sake, what is it?" She could hear her mother running downstairs and Stephen running upstairs. But nobody came to her door. Then she heard Stephen shout, "What? Are you sure?" And her mother's answer, breathless and inaudible. And then

Stephen again saying, "Which way?" And both foot-steps hurrying downstairs. And then Stephen saying, "Wait. Close the kitchen door. Then we can catch it."

It! What was it? Julie sat up and looked over at the couch. No cat! It! The cat! Now she understood. Con-sternation propelled Julie out of bed and into the hall. Though her eyes were not quite adjusted to the light, she started toward the stairs.

"Wait!" she called out. "I'll find it." She almost tripped on the top step as she hurried down. When she got to the kitchen, she saw Stephen standing there holding the cat disdainfully out in front of him as though it was a dirty rag. She paused for a minute before anyone saw her. What were they thinking? What should she do? Now she was really in trouble, especially with Stephen. Her mother was sitting at the table, half-laughing in a relieved way.

"I thought it was something much worse," she was saying, "a rat or something."

"But how . . . ?" Stephen was saying.

"And in Julie's room," her mother added. "I can't guess how it got there. Unless it got up on the porch roof and in the window."

The cat was beginning to squirm out of Stephen's unfriendly grasp. "Here, Marjorie," he said, "open the door. We'll figure it all out later," he continued as Mom stood up and started toward the door. "Let's get rid of—"

"Wait," said Julie. "Wait. I'll take it." Mom and Stephen turned toward her.

"Julie!" said Mom.

"Julie," said Stephen, "do you know anything about

this cat?" From the expression on his face he might as well have said, "So you're the guilty party!"

With both of them looking at her, Julie suddenly realized that she was standing there in nothing but her nightgown. Not that it showed anything. It was a heavy winter nightgown with a high neck and long sleeves. But since she and Mom had started living with Stephen, she had made sure that Stephen saw her fully clothed or with her bathrobe on. Now she was protected by only one layer of pale, pink flannel from Stephen's accusing eyes.

"Why, Julie," said her mother, "do you know where the cat came from?"

"It's a stray," said Julie. "Some kid left it on our street and moved to Chicago."

"That's a strange thing to do," said her mother.

Stephen had stopped holding the cat in front of him and was holding it in his arms, where it had settled down comfortably. "It seems too friendly to be a stray," said Stephen.

"It's always hanging around," said Julie, "as though it has no place to go." For one moment Julie allowed herself the wild, improbable hope that Stephen would want to keep the cat. When he stood there holding it . . . . Could she fit him into the picture at Mrs. Mitchell's door? The one that said, "Like a Shepherd."

"That doesn't prove it's a stray," he said. "That yellow cat's always stalking the bird feeder, but I know it belongs to someone in the neighborhood. It gets fatter every day, and I hope it's not on birds. Somebody must be feeding it. You haven't fed this one, have you? Not a little bit of milk or something?"

"No," said Julie.

"Well, that's good. Once you feed a stray cat, it's yours forever."

"But if it's a stray," said Julie, "maybe no one's feeding it."

"Julie," said her mother gently, but sternly, "I think you might have let us know that you had a cat in your room."

Why didn't parents use their heads? If you hid something from them, you always had a good reason. Because Stephen doesn't like cats. She could say that. Which was the real reason. "Because I thought you wouldn't like it," she said, looking mainly at Stephen.

"But we would have known in the morning," said her mother.

"I was going to let it go before you woke up," said Julie. It made her sound so calculating. From the way she was frowning, Julie knew that was what Mom was thinking. She's wondering if I'm going to become a juvenile delinquent and start shoplifting and taking dope. Ordinarily, Julie never did anything deceptive. No wonder Mom couldn't figure it out.

"I think it's time for the cat to go," said Stephen.

"Not outside," said Julie. "It might catch a chill and die." She started toward him to take the cat away.

"Why not the back porch?" said her mother, coming over and kissing Julie on the cheek. "Julie must promise to let it out first thing in the morning."

"Well . . ." said Stephen. "Well, I don't think it's a good plan." Mom gave him a look. It was a look that meant, I'll discuss it with you later. Julie didn't care what they said together in the double bed that night as long as the cat was protected from the rain.

"Thanks, Mom," said Julie. Lucky her mother was on her side. Stephen was already opening the door. Julie wanted to say good night to the cat, but not with Mom and Stephen standing around. After Stephen closed the door behind him, Julie could see his head appear at the window of the door and then suddenly disappear. He's trying to get in without letting the cat in, Julie thought.

"Good night, dear," said her mother, kissing her on the cheek again. "Chasing cats makes me sleepy. Tell Steve I've gone up." Between the two of them, Mom and Stephen had worked it out. And I got what I wanted, thought Julie, almost . . . . What she really wanted, getting to keep the cat, "is impossible," she said to herself.

She saw Stephen's head again and this time the whole of Stephen came through the door like light-ning and banged it shut behind him. Did he need to bang it quite so hard? Suppose he caught the cat's tail in the door? Julie listened, and Stephen seemed to listen too, but there was no anguished "*meow.*"

"Damn nuisance," Stephen muttered and he looked toward Julie. Me, or the cat, or both, Julie thought. She looked back at Stephen, filling the silence with her own thoughts. If you weren't here, I'd have a cat, she thought resentfully. Actually, if you weren't here, I wouldn't be here either and therefore I wouldn't have a cat. It was hard to blame everything on Stephen. Mainly she wished she had more control over what happened to her.

"Night," said Stephen. "Take it down to the end of

the driveway in the morning," he said, "so it doesn't hang around the birds."

He's not thinking about me at all, Julie concluded. Only the usual—birds and my mom. At least there was something bracing about facing things honestly, like the feeling of the sharp air when she opened the door onto the back porch. In the light shining from the kitchen, she could see the cat over in the corner.

"Here, kitty," she called. "I can't stay long. Here, Nuisance," she called, half-laughing, to the cat. It responded to the name and came over to rub its warm, furry body against her cold ankles.

"I'll be back in the morning," she promised as she checked to make sure the outside door was locked. "Don't go away, Nuisance," she said, patting the cat's head. "We need each other." Then she carried Nuisance to the far corner of the porch, crossed quickly back, and slipped into the kitchen.

The Spell

"I haven't seen the cat since," said Julie. "Have you?"
She was sitting on the front steps of Cal's house,
watching Cal and Captain Crunch put together the
afternoon papers. Julie had walked home from school
alone that day because Cynthia and Rosalie stayed for
the meeting, the one about the Valentine's Dance.

"It's only a few days away and there's so much to do.
Why don't you help?" Rosalie had suggested.

"I might not go," said Julie.

"Oh, you have to, honey," Cynthia insisted. "That's
the way to meet people. And besides, you're supposed
to lure Cal Winston there."

"Not much chance of that," said Julie. "But I'll see.
I'll see you tomorrow." And she left.

She was in a hurry. She walked fast, almost ran. She
was determined to reach Cal before he left to deliver
newspapers. Across East-West Highway. Down the
path between the houses. Along Raymond Street.
When she saw Cal working on the newspapers, she
slowed down, hesitant about going right up to him.
After all, she didn't really know him very well. But in a
way she did. A snow day and a bicycle accident helped
you get to know people quickly. The past week had he
been avoiding her? Or was it Cynthia and Rosalie?

"Hey, Jewel! What's new?" Cal called. That was her

answer. Julie crossed the street to talk with Cal and
then Captain Crunch came out of the house to help
him. Then Julie sat down on the top step. The sun was
so warm that she unzipped her winter jacket. None of
them wore mittens and for the second time she saw
Cal without a cap on. There were the red-brown curls
that she had given up looking for in the halls at school.
Friendly, gentle curls, she thought, imagining how
springy they would feel if one were to put one's hand
on his head as he bent over the newspapers.

"I can't believe it," Julie said.

"I don't believe that," said Cal. "You'll believe anything."

"Only three days ago it was cold and rainy," Julie
continued. "That was when Nuisance . . . ." She
paused. Would they think it was a silly name for a cat?
No sillier than Captain Crunch for a boy or Jewel . . . .
When Cal called her Jewel, it felt just right, like a soft,
sparkly veil being thrown over her hair. Maybe the cat
didn't like being called Nuisance. Maybe that's why it
had disappeared.

"Nuisance who?" said Cal matter-of-factly.

"Nuisance, the cat," said Julie, and she told Cal and
Captain Crunch about The Cat Episode.

Captain Crunch's eyes were wide and he said
"Wow!" when Julie told about the banging door.
When she told about Stephen chasing the cat around
the house, he and Cal both laughed. "Weren't you in
trouble?" asked Captain Crunch.

"Of course not, child," said Cal loftily. "Jewel is a
princess and princesses are never in trouble. Everyone
has to do what Jewel tells them to do."

"Did your parents let you keep it?" asked Captain Crunch skeptically.

"My mom and . . ."—what should she call Stephen? —"they didn't believe it was a stray cat. So they made me let it go the next morning." No point in getting into the subject of Stephen's birds.

"But I explained it all to Your Highness," said Cal. "If Your Highness would like, I would be glad to repeat the explanation to your royal parents."

"I don't think it would help," said Julie, but she didn't go on to say why. If she started talking about Stephen and birds, she might end up telling the whole story in spite of herself. Sometimes she felt it was like a stream damned up inside her that some day was going to burst out against her will.

"Are you sure Captain Crunch was right?" asked Julie. "They said we couldn't be sure. That it was just some kid's story. And they also said they were glad I hadn't fed it, because if you feed a cat it keeps coming back. Maybe it really does belong to somebody else. Because I haven't seen the cat since," said Julie. "Have you?"

"No," said Cal. "Not a whisker." The papers were done, and he sat down on the step next to Julie. "Whew! We're having a heat wave," he said as he took off his jacket. Julie liked the color of his sweater. It was dark green, the green of Christmas trees.

"Maybe winter's over," Captain Crunch said breathlessly. He was bouncing a super-ball on the pavement and scrambling to catch it.

"I wish it was," said Julie. "Then I wouldn't have to worry about Nuisance freezing to death."

"Now look here, Princess Jewel," said Cal. "If you

want the cat back, tell me, and I'll do a spell right this minute that'll make it reappear."

"Your spell didn't work on my ribbon snake," said Captain Crunch, catching a particularly high bounce. "It's been gone since Christmas."

"It's true, I did say a week," Cal agreed. "That's the usual time for spells. But sometimes they take longer than one expects. Magic can't be forced, you know."

"Dad says we're going to find it in the basement in a couple of years. All big—miles and miles long."

"You mistrust my magic powers?" Cal stood up to catch the super-ball and bounce it back at Captain Crunch. "I do, hereby now before these witnesses," he said, waving his right arm, "proclaim that I will make the Royal Princess Jewel's cat, Nuisance, reappear."

"Here? Now?" asked Captain Crunch.

"No, child," said Cal. "You are too impatient. I told you, great magic takes time."

"Then when?" asked Julie, looking up at Cal. Standing there with his arm outstretched, he looked very tall and strong, as though he could do anything.

"Where?" asked Captain Crunch.

"Within a week from this very day on Her Highness's back porch, the cat, Nuisance, will reappear.

> Cats, bats, rats, gnats,
> Hocus, pocus, wearing hats.
> Hocus, pocus, wearing hats,
> Gnats, rats, bats, cats."

Cal collapsed next to Julie as though exhausted from the exercise of his magical powers.

"Wow!" said Captain Crunch. "That was a good spell."

"Okay, Jewel," Cal said, putting his arm around her shoulders. "Go home and prepare to greet your wandering cat. While I, in the disguise of a wizard, will deliver the newspapers." His arm was only there for a moment, like a light, brief visit of a butterfly, but it communicated to Julie a shock of energy that made her blush. Did Cal notice it too? He stood up abruptly and said, "Now, slave, load the newspapers onto the chariot."

"You mean me?" said Captain Crunch. "You mean the bicycle?"

"Forsooth, lad, but you're a lazy oaf."

"Here, I'll help," said Julie, standing up.

"Nay, Jewel," said Cal, "this is no work for a princess." But he let her help, and Captain Crunch helped too.

"So, I leap onto my steed, thus," said Cal, "and—" He was about wave a gallant farewell when he looked beyond Julie and his arm dropped.

"Good-bye," he said hastily and cycled off. He looked almost scared. Was it the witch? Was it Mrs. Mitchell? Julie turned around and saw Cynthia and Rosalie walking toward her.

"Think it'll work?" Captain Crunch was pulling on her arm. It was like the feeling of a dream pulling at her after she was awake.

"Hi, Julie," Cynthia called out. Like a dream, Captain Crunch vanished into the house.

"Now we know why you couldn't stay," said Rosalie.

"In a way," said Julie, "but not exactly."

"Why don't you come back and have a Coke with us?" said Cynthia.

"And tell us everything," said Rosalie.

"Sure," said Julie. "I'll put my books on the back porch." She started to run up the driveway.

"Take your time, honey," said Cynthia.

Julie walked and thought. Tell us everything, Rosalie had said. She let the porch door bang behind her, put her books down on the chair by the door, and stood for a moment. To tell about something sometimes meant you lost it. She would leave the memory of Cal's arm around her shoulders hidden with her books on the porch, to be taken out and cherished later. When they asked her about Cal, she would act as though nothing special had happened.

"No, balloons are best," Cynthia was saying when she got back. "They're easiest and cheapest."

"Dullsville. We have them at every dance," Rosalie complained.

"Because they're easy and cheap," Cynthia insisted.

The discussion about decorations lasted until Cynthia's house. Julie hoped maybe the girls had forgotten about Cal. But when they were sitting in Cynthia's kitchen drinking Cokes and listening to "Every Woman in the World," Rosalie said, "Cal's really shy."

"You might be the only girl he's talked to," said Cynthia.

"We've been trying to get to know him since kindergarten," said Rosalie.

"We think he's cute," said Cynthia.

"What'd you talk about?" asked Rosalie.

How could she answer them? Now she understood why Cal ignored her when she was with them. It wasn't that he was shy. Not with her, anyhow. It was that he didn't think Cynthia and Rosalie would understand his language. He didn't feel comfortable calling them funny names or princesses or making up spells for them.

"Nothing much," Julie said.

"What we've been trying to do for years, you did in a month," said Cynthia.

"I didn't do anything," said Julie. "I hardly ever see him." The protective words slid out effortlessly.

"If he knows you're coming to the dance, maybe he'll come too," said Cynthia.

"I don't think it would make any difference."

"Have you told him?" asked Rosalie.

"I haven't decided. Remember?"

"You have to come!" they both said together.

"Why wouldn't you?" asked Rosalie.

Why? How much should she tell them? They seemed like older sisters, interfering, officious, but knowledgeable and good natured.

"Because I've never been to one and I wouldn't know what to do." Now, would they forever turn their backs on her ignorance?

If Rosalie was shocked, she concealed it. "Well, you've got to start some time."

"Ye-e-e-ss." Julie was thinking, Do I? Life was much less complicated back in Virginia.

"We'll tell you what to do, honey," said Cynthia.

"And what to wear," said Rosalie.

"And if Cal came . . . " said Cynthia.

If he was invisible at school, he was probably invisible at dances too. But suppose he wasn't. Then Julie wanted to be there. For sure.

"Okay," she said. "I'll try it."

"Let Cal know you're going," said Rosalie as they walked back together.

"If I get a chance," Julie muttered. She thought how much fun it would be to look forward to the dance knowing for certain that Cal was going to be there. But then she thought of the hidden memory, his arm on her shoulder as quick and light as a butterfly. And as easily frightened, she thought. I won't say anything about the dance, she resolved.

For a while they walked along in silence. It was getting dark. The winter chill that was stored deep down in the earth rose up to meet them like a pent-up evil spirit. Julie looked on all the porches, down all the driveways, and in all the front yards for a gray-striped tabby cat with white paws. In case, she thought to herself, Cal's spell has worked already.

"You haven't changed your mind?" asked Rosalie. "You're still coming Friday night?"

Julie couldn't keep herself from glancing over toward Cal's house. "If it's okay with my mom," she said, hoping Rosalie hadn't noticed. "Bye," she said as she started up the driveway. The light was on and she could smell something cooking, something with onions. It would be nice to find her mom there waiting for her, for once.

Before she went in, she walked around the yard to make sure there was no sign of the cat. "Kitty," she called. "Nuisance," she called. "Are you there?" The thawed grass was spongy underfoot. How would it feel if one had paws?

Julie looked behind the garage. There was a space between the woodpile and the garage wall that would be perfect for a cat to squeeze into. Were those white paws behind that log? She knelt down to investigate.

"Nuisance," she called. And she reached into the shadows. How warm a furry cat would feel against her cold hands! But the white spots were only some rough bits of dried fungus.

Julie stood up. The cold seemed to come from the ground, from the sky, from the icy woodpile. "I hope you're somewhere warm," said Julie. "I hope you aren't out in the cold." Mom and Stephen were probably right, Julie thought as she walked back to the house. At night Nuisance probably did have a home to go to after wandering around the neighborhood during the day. And then little kids were easy to fool. Maybe that other kid was only fooling Captain Crunch with his story about moving to Chicago.

But if it turned out to be a stray after all? Julie left her wet shoes on the porch and picked up her books. She followed the onion smell into the kitchen.

"Hello, dear," her mother called from the living room.

"Hi, Mom," said Julie, looking through the window of the lighted oven. Meat loaf and baked potatoes. If Cal's spell worked and Nuisance came back? As Julie carried her books up to her room, thoughts of the cat changed to memories of Cal.

The Dance

"As a pet, you're much simpler to take care of than a cat," Julie said to the rabbit fern while she watered it. "Will you wait up for me tonight?" she said. "It'll be late when I get home from the dance." Her mother and Stephen wouldn't be there. Since they were going to a party, they would probably get back even later. "I'll tell you all about it," she said, turning toward the mirror to look at herself. She had half an hour still before Mom drove her over to the dance with Cynthia and Rosalie. Afterward, Cynthia's dad was going to bring them all home.

"Will anyone dance with me?" she asked herself. "Will I know what to do if anyone does?" Her brown eyes looked sober and anxious. "Don't look so worried," she admonished herself. But her hands felt clammy.

"Wear jeans," Rosalie had advised her. "Everyone does."

"Designer jeans," Cynthia had said.

"New jeans for a dance!" Mom couldn't understand it. "Shouldn't you wear a dress?" she asked. But she did get Julie some clogs and a bright red turtleneck. Mom seemed to be enjoying the preparations. "Your first dance," she kept saying. Julie felt close to her again, as though they were back in Virginia, just the two of them again.

"And you need eye shadow," Rosalie had said.

"I haven't got any." Julie felt as though all her sins were laid bare to Cynthia and Rosalie.

"That's all right. I'll bring some and you can put it on in the girls' room."

"Eye shadow will make all the difference," Cynthia had added.

Julie checked her digital clock—8:05. Then 8:06. Then finally minute by minute it was 8:39. At last. "I'd better go find Mom," she said to the clock. "I hope Cal comes," she said to her reflection.

How could it be so cold so suddenly? Julie wondered as she ran from the back door to the car. Her clogs struck against the frosty bricks like wooden chimes.

"Turn on the heater," she said as soon as she got in. She was shivering with cold and nervousness.

"I will, dear, as soon as the engine warms up," her mother soothed, patting her hand. Mom, just her mom alone, was really understanding.

"Hello," her mother said as Cynthia got into the backseat. "Are you all ready for the dance?"

"Yes, ma'am," said Cynthia.

"Is this your first—?" she said.

"Oh, Mom," said Julie.

"Your first dance this year," her mother continued calmly.

"No, ma'am," said Cynthia. "We had a Harvest Dance and a Christmas Dance." Cynthia didn't say anything more, but sat quietly in the shadowy backseat. When Julie looked around, she could see the top of her blond head shining in the light that came in the rear window. She smiled at Cynthia, but she couldn't think of anything to say. Is Cynthia worried, she wondered, the way I am? About who's going to dance with her?

"Now which house is it?" her mother asked. They had turned onto Rosalie's street.

"The next one on the left," said Cynthia, "with the lantern out front." Her voice sounded bottled up. She is worried, Julie decided. Why would anyone as beautiful as Cynthia, who had been to dances before, need to worry? Perhaps it was something one never got over, like stage fright.

When Rosalie finally swept into the car, she brought with her the aura of musk and the clink of bangles.

"I have it," she told Julie in a resonant whisper as she got in. The eye shadow! Julie looked guiltily at her mother, but she didn't seem to notice. With Rosalie in the car, Cynthia brightened up and they chattered and giggled all the way to school. They talked about the boys they hoped would dance with them and the boys they hoped wouldn't dance with them. They said things Julie would never have said in front of her own mother, even though she was really understanding.

"I wrote down our number at the party," she reminded Julie as the girls got out of the car. "Don't forget to call when you get back. You've got your key?"

"Yes, Mom."

"Lock the door as soon as you go in. And"—her mother seemed to search for the right thing to say—"have fun."

"Thanks," said Julie. "You too," she said and

thought how lucky Mom was to be going with Stephen
—someone who would take care of her at the party.
And if there hadn't been a Stephen to go to parties
with, then Mom would be waiting for her when she got
home, or there to call if she wanted to come home
early.

Julie looked toward her mother's car, disappearing
out of the school driveway, and then toward the
lighted school building, where groups of kids were
going in and out of the big front door, while one
group was trying to climb in the window of a first floor
classroom. Julie stood there alone. Cynthia and Rosalie must have gone in while she was saying good-bye
to her mother. Everybody else seemed to be a part of
something. And she had no choice now but to go and
be a part of something too. I'm caught, Julie thought
as she followed a group of older boys in the front
door. But it was my own choice, she added, which
somehow made it better.

"There you are," said Rosalie, pulling at her arm. "I
thought you were with us. Come on, I've got eye
shadow, and rouge, and mascara."

They pushed through the crowd in the girls' room
to a quiet corner. "Oooh, you've got sequined socks,"
someone was squealing. Julie sat on the radiator while
Rosalie laid several little boxes and brushes on the
windowsill. She looked at Rosalie's intent face as she
lined her eyebrows and brushed mascara on her
eyelashes.

"Don't blink," said Rosalie. Her own eyelashes were
already thick with mascara.

What would Cal say, Julie wondered, if he saw me

looking like that? Then there was the eye shadow and the rouge.

"Now," said Rosalie triumphantly, "look at yourself!" Julie stood on tiptoe behind the girls who had been parked in front of the mirror for the last half hour.

"Is that me?" she said to the apparition with dark, devouring eyes, hovering behind their faces.

"Hey, Julie, you look neat," said one of the girls, without turning.

"I do, I guess," said Julie, looking in the mirror to see who was speaking. It was the girl from her homeroom, Mary, her boxes and pots on the shelf in front of her, working on her face with the concentration of a great artist. There was nothing left of the real Mary. Her face was just a painting. Julie rubbed at the rouge on her own face, which seemed obviously fake, but left the mysterious eyes intact.

"Now don't touch a thing," said Rosalie behind her.

"Thanks," siad Julie. "You were swell to do it."

"Rosalie, I've been looking for you," someone called in the bathroom door. Rosalie was gone before Julie could catch up with her and Julie was again left on her own. Since the girls in front of the next mirror had drifted away, she went over to look at herself once more.

"You've got to help," she said, leaning toward herself, but the dark eyes glared back unsympathetically.

When she went out into the hall, she saw Wilma hesitating by the coatrack. Julie was surprised. Why would such a quiet girl come to a dance? She's probably surprised to see me too, thought Julie. Everyone else seemed to be going somewhere and nobody looked familiar.

"Hi," she said to Wilma.

Wilma started. "Oh, it's you, Julie," she said. Julie noticed that she didn't have any makeup on, which made Julie feel superior.

"This is my first," Julie paused, "dance at this school," she said. It sounded as though she'd been to a million dances back in Virginia. What was it about dances that made one pretend to be what one wasn't? Not like Cal's pretending. His pretending was a way of saying things he really felt and wanted. But this pretending was a way of concealing what one really was and felt in order to make one seem more self-assured.

Cal! She looked up and down the hall. If she saw him, she thought she'd run back into the girls' bathroom. She couldn't reconcile the Julie she was trying to be now with the person he called Jewel.

"We might as well . . . " Wilma was saying.

"What?" said Julie.

"Go into the dance," said Wilma, as though she had said the same thing a minute before.

"Sure," said Julie. It was nice to have someone to be with, even someone as mousy as Wilma. Together they followed the thud, thud, thud of the rock music down the hall toward the gym.

"I'm glad I met you," confided Wilma. "I don't like to go into a dance alone."

"Neither do I," said Julie, and she felt relieved to be honest.

When Julie stepped into the gym, she wondered if anything was real in this world of writhing, ghoulish creatures.

"Wait till you see the lighting," Rosalie had said. "You'll really freak out." That kind of talk made Julie think of drugs.

"You mean just over lights?" Julie had said. She was worried that somehow, despite her caution, by going to the dance, she would be drawn into the underworld of drugs.

"Yes, just lights." Rosalie had seemed insulted, as though she had guessed Julie's suspicions. You had to be careful of what you said to friends until you'd known each other long enough to feel secure.

Julie reached out and touched Wilma. In this strange setting, she wanted to be sure Wilma was there. She felt safe enough with Wilma. Her manner was quiet, but she wasn't hiding anything. If either of them freaked out, it would only be over the lights. The lights and the music.

"What d'you think?" she shouted in Wilma's ear. Thud, thud, thud. She couldn't even hear herself.

"Weird," Wilma shouted. And then she said something more from which Julie heard "always." She seemed more talkative than usual, but Julie couldn't hear most of what she said.

The beams of blue-and-red spots crisscrossed in the center of the room, creating a pool of deep purple light in which dancers' arms and legs were flung about like separate creatures. Hanging from the ceiling in the center of the room, a faceted, mirrored ball turned silently, sprinkling circles of light like golden coins around the room. Julie couldn't see any balloons. Rosalie must have thought of using the light instead.

Everything is light and sound and nobody exists, not even me, thought Julie. In a way, it was a release

not to exist. Mascara, rouge, it was all irrelevent. If Cal
came, it wouldn't matter, Julie thought. I'd never find
him, and if I did, I wouldn't know him and he wouldn't
know me. But she kept looking at the kids around her,
boys, girls, she could hardly tell which, for someone
tall with round glasses and curls sticking out all over.

Julie followed Wilma to the group of girls over on
the side who were waiting to be asked to dance. Even
though this was her first dance, Julie saw the group for
what it was: extinction. If you didn't get asked to dance
right away, you got lost in this group unless some very
determined person came and rescued you. And it
would be so hard to find anyone in the dark mass.

"Let's stand over here," shouted Julie, moving to
the far edge of the group. That way she would be
available without looking too lonely and exposed. The
music thrummed on and there was no need or opportunity for conversation. One didn't even need to smile
if one didn't feel like it. Nobody could tell.

Julie had just reached the despairing conclusion
that she was going to spend the entire evening without
dancing when a voice out of the shadows grumbled
something at her that sounded like, "Wanna dance?"

Julie knew right away it wasn't Cal. Not from anything she could see or hear. She simply knew. After
that, it didn't matter who it was, only that it was somebody. As she moved toward the voice, she started to
discern his face in the scattered light. It was The Brain
—Arnold Finch. That was another surprise. Julie
thought brains didn't do sociable things like dance,
but Arnold Finch was one that apparently did.

Julie blessed the anonymity of the darkly throbbing

room. There was no question of "doing it right." No
one would know whether you did. The important
thing was to do something in time to the music facing
the person who was your partner. Beyond that, everyone appeared to be moving in his or her own, random,
personal way.

"You're not bad," Arnold shouted after a few minutes. Not bad at what? Dancing? Math?

"Thanks," shouted Julie. She wasn't sure whether
he heard her. That was all he said. He seemed really
involved, throwing himself around. Then after several
dances, he disappeared as abruptly and mysteriously
as he had come. Julie was sorry to stop. She loved the
rhythmic abandon of dancing. Without a partner,
there was nothing to do but merge back into the group
of onlookers. Wilma wasn't there. Julie thought she
saw her out dancing with another girl. At least she'd
gotten to dance with a boy. No one glamorous, but he
was a boy.

Wilma came back and they stood together a while
longer. It was getting tiresome to stand and watch and
not be a part of the uninhibited motion. Wilma pulled
at Julie's arm.

"What?" Julie leaned toward her.

"Let's eat!" Wilma had to make an effort to shout.

Julie nodded her head and with a last look at the
dance floor turned to follow Wilma to the refreshment
room. As she turned, she saw a boy and girl, separate
from the others, dancing in the purple light.

"That's Rosalie!" She could tell by the bangles,
which reflected the light as she raised her arms. "I've
finally recognized someone." And the boy with her?

Julie wished she hadn't looked. He had round, metal-rimmed glasses. It must be Cal. Cal! And Rosalie had got to him before Julie even knew he was there. He certainly wasn't invisible at dances. He wasn't even shy at dances.

Julie looked toward the door where Wilma was waiting. How can I get home, how can I leave right away? she thought. If only Cal hadn't come at all. She forced herself to turn back to look once more, to make herself remember why she would *never* go to a dance again. Why she would never speak to Cal again.

The dancers had changed position and Rosalie and Cal were much closer to her now. Since his back was toward her, though, he couldn't see her. As circles of mirrored light rained down on him, she watched his head jerking back and forth in time to the music. But his hair wasn't curly. No, not one curl.

Julie peered again through the dark till the light showered over him once more. The hair was straight! Straight, dark hair. It wasn't Cal. Cal's hair was silly curls all over the place. And he was too short for Cal anyhow.

"I knew you wouldn't," she said out loud, because no one could hear her. "I knew you wouldn't be dumb enough to come to a dumb dance like this." And yet she still hoped he had come, guessing, without her having said anything, that she would be there. Maybe he didn't dance. Maybe he only ate. Perhaps he had been waiting for her all this time to come out for refreshments. Julie ran to join Wilma, who was still standing at the door.

The refreshment tables set up in the hall outside the

gym were lit by the usual, everyday, dim overhead bulbs. But by comparison with the gym, the lights over the tables seemed blindingly bright. Despite the mascara and the rouge, Julie felt revealed, unmasked, as she stood sipping punch. Everyone could see that she wasn't dancing and that she was talking with a girl, not a boy.

In *True Romance,* at a moment like this, the "person you had been waiting for" always came up from behind and whispered, "Julie," passionately. "Jewel." That's what Cal would whisper. Julie looked around. First at the students hanging over the two tables and then at the clusters strung out along the hall. From what she could observe, Cal wasn't there. She looked intently for a few more minutes as groups shifted and people she hadn't seen before became visible. No sign of Cal. And if he wasn't at the dance by now, he probably wasn't coming. He had left her to survive her first dance alone. Julie found herself feeling unreasonably angry with him, as though he'd promised to be there and hadn't shown up.

Instead of seeing Cal, she saw Mrs. Barker, who was talking with two of the parent chaperones, looking over toward her. She hoped she didn't show how forlorn she felt. A C-minus in math and nobody to dance with. That was failure. How could she fill the time until Cynthia's dad came? She hated the thought of rejoining the group of eager, anonymous girls massed at the side of the dance floor.

"You been living around here long?" She tried to get a conversation going with Wilma.

"Yes," said Wilma, and that was all.

Julie could see Mrs. Barker nodding to the parents and starting over in her direction. I wish I could impress her with something I've done, thought Julie, instead of always needing help.

"Hello, Wilma. Hello, Julie," said Mrs. Barker. "I'm glad you came. It takes some courage at a new school." And she did sound impressed. She reached over for a cup of punch. "My goodness, this table's a mess," she said. "I don't know what happened to the students on the refreshment committee." Which included Cynthia, Julie remembered.

"I'll help," she volunteered. Then she could stop looking like a failure and start looking like someone on the refreshment committee.

First, she piled up dirty cups. "Thank you, dear," said one of the mothers. Then she and Wilma refilled the potato chip bowls. It was something to do, but she was jealous of Cynthia, who was obviously having so much fun somewhere in the depths of the gym that she couldn't tear herself away.

Mary came in with two boys. They both looked like ninth graders, the smooth kind that were on the football team. What I need to be a success is more makeup, Julie concluded after studying Mary's face.

"Aren't you dancing?" Mary seemed shocked. How could someone wearing mascara not be dancing? "Scott," she said, giving one of the boys a shove, "take Julie in and dance with her. She's new and doesn't know anyone."

Scott looked as though he wanted to say, "That kid? Forget it." Instead, he put his arm around Julie's waist and guided her onto the dance floor.

"Back in a minute, baby doll," he called to Mary.

It wasn't as much fun dancing with someone who had been conscripted to be her partner. On the other hand, if the girls on the side could see her, they'd be impressed that she was dancing with this handsome ninth grader, a big advance from Arnold Finch. And if Cal saw her? Would he be jealous? As Julie got more into the feeling of the music, she stopped thinking about how anyone else was reacting. The dance seemed to go quickly. She was sorry when Scott said, "Let's get some more refreshments."

"Thanks," said Julie. It had been nice of him to dance with her.

When they got back to the refreshment room, Mary and the other boy had left. "What a stinking dame," said Scott and rushed down the hall to look for them. Did Mary use her to get away from Scott, or what? She looked toward Wilma, who was stacking dirty paper cups, for an answer to the question she hadn't asked out loud.

"Do you know where Mary went?" she asked instead.

"No," said Wilma. "I wasn't watching. I'm sorry."

"That's okay," said Julie. It was really Mary's problem if she wanted to act that way, Julie told herself. But she still felt chagrined at the thought that Mary might have been using her. She had a lot to learn about dances.

"I'll be right back," she told Wilma, who was mopping up a puddle of punch from the floor. At the moment, the girls' bathroom seemed like an appealing haven.

Looking into the mirror, she saw the little girl, Julie, wearing her big sister's mascara. "It doesn't make you more attractive," she told Julie. "Not even to boys like Scott." How all the kids must be laughing at the way Mary had duped Julie Howard into duping Scott for her.

A group of ninth-grade girls came in. "If he thinks he's going to score with me . . ." one of them was saying. Then they all looked at Julie as though they wished she would leave. So she did. What does that mean? she wondered as she walked back to the refreshment table. She could guess, but when there was no one around she asked Wilma.

"Do you know what 'score' means?"

"In what?" said Wilma.

"Between boys and girls," said Julie.

"No," she said. She looked frightened, the way she did when Arnold Finch asked her questions.

"I didn't think you would," said Julie. "Neither do I." It was like being at home with Stephen and Mom. People were active and preoccupied in ways that excluded her. There was only one way she would have felt a part of everything. That was if Cal had come. As she pushed through the kids who were standing around snacking on potato chips to collect the dirty cups, she found herself thinking about Cal—what the dance would have been like if he had come, if he had appeared in the dark, raucous gym and started dancing with her, grinning at her while his curls bounced up and down.

"That's the way, Jewel," she could imagine him encouraging her. Where was he at this moment? she wondered. Was he at home with Captain Crunch, watching TV? Just because he wasn't at the dance didn't mean he couldn't be somewhere else with . . . a girl. Cal. Julie stood still for a moment and thought about him very hard. Wherever you are, Cal, I miss you. That was the message she sent him.

"Time to clear up," said one of the mothers. Julie and Wilma helped to carry out the punch bowls, which only had ice left in them. As they carried out the potato chip bowls, they finished up the salty crumbs at the bottom.

Cynthia arrived breathless and apologetic. "Refreshments! I was so worried. I kept trying to get here. But Tony's a real caveman. Every time I tried to leave, he dragged me to the other side of the room. Oh, yes, my dad's waiting."

At last, thought Julie. "Good-bye, Wilma," she said. "See you on Monday."

"Thanks a lot, honey, for helping out in my place," said Cynthia as they walked down the hall to get their coats. "I hope you didn't spend the whole evening eating." Julie could feel the air getting colder as they moved closer to the door.

"No, I danced," said Julie defensively. "It was fun." And it was, the dancing part. She hoped Cynthia hadn't noticed about Mary and Scott.

"Did you see Cal?" Rosalie asked when they met her at the door.

"Was he here?" Julie tried to speak calmly. It must have been Cal dancing with Rosalie after all.

"I didn't see him," said Rosalie. "I thought you might have." Another false alarm.

Although they didn't reproach her, Julie somehow felt apologetic toward Cynthia and Rosalie that Cal hadn't come to the dance. Silly, she scolded herself. They had plenty of other boys to dance with.

Since Cynthia sat in front with her dad, she and Rosalie couldn't talk much during the drive home.

"Meet anyone interesting?" Rosalie asked Julie.

"Not really, did you?"

"There was one cute guy," Rosalie said. Julie wondered if it had been the boy with the round glasses and the straight hair.

"Call you tomorrow," said Cynthia when Rosalie got out of the car. "Bye, honey," she said to Julie when Julie got out.

"Thanks for the lift," said Julie.

"Want me to wait?" asked Cynthia's dad.

Julie knew that was what her mother would like, but she was anxious to separate herself as quickly as possible from everything connected with the dance. And from the way Cynthia's dad accelerated the engine, she decided he was in a hurry.

"I'm okay," she said. "I've got a key."

The roar of the car pulling away sounded the final theme of a disappointing evening. What was left but the dreary conclusion of going into the house alone, calling her mother, and getting into bed?

Are You Saved?

Julie stood for a moment at the foot of the driveway before she went up. From the outside, her house looked bright and welcoming. Her mother had left the lights on in almost all the rooms. But she felt strange about going into an empty house late at night, after eleven o'clock.

She looked over at Cal's house. Could she tell whether he was home? There was a light on in a second-floor room. Was that Cal's bedroom? Captain Crunch would be asleep by now and his parents would still be downstairs. Someone was there, at least, watching TV. Julie could see the blue light from the screen. Was Cal upstairs in bed reading *Sports Illustrated* or a magazine about bicycles?

Otherwise, all was still and quiet along the street. Mrs. Mitchell's house was black with the black points of the evergreens silhouetted above it. Is she in bed already, Julie speculated, or is she out riding on her broomstick?

Julie didn't feel very nervous as she turned to walk up the driveway to the back of the house because it was well lit with moonlight. There was something exciting and energizing about being out so late alone, moving like a swimmer through the channel of cold moonlight that flowed down the driveway. The back-porch light was on and the porch door was slightly open.

"Whew! Is it cold!" said Julie to herself as she stepped inside.

"Meow," said a little voice. Julie looked down. There was Nuisance standing at the kitchen door waiting for her.

"Nuisance!" Julie said.

"Meow?" said Nuisance, as though it were a question.

"Of course I'm glad to see you, you dear, wonderful cat," said Julie as though she were answering a question.

In the same affectionate manner as before, Nuisance started to rub against Julie's legs. That little bit of cat warmth seemed to creep through Julie's jeans right up to her heart. Nuisance appeared so dependent and trusting. It made Julie feel important and helpless.

"But I'll find a way, Nuisance," said Julie, taking off her glove and kneeling down on the cold porch floor to stroke the cat. "I'll find a way to help you. Maybe not tonight, but as soon as I can." She took off her other glove and picked Nuisance up so that she could hold the precious little body in her arms. What had once seemed awkward now seemed easy.

"Cal's spell worked," she whispered in Nuisance's ear. "Just wait till I tell him."

When her knees got too cold and sore, she grabbed a newspaper from the pile in the box and sat down on it. Then she lifted the cat into her lap.

"You don't belong to anyone," she said to Nuisance, "at least not anymore or you wouldn't be out on a night like this."

Nuisance managed to curl up comfortably in the curve of her legs and began to purr. "But you mustn't get too settled," said Julie, "because I can't let you stay. Not tonight. Not ever, probably." Julie stroked and Nuisance purred. The inexorable cold seeped, layer by layer, through her jacket and her red turtleneck, through her skin and flesh into her bones.

"If I can't stand it, how can you?" Julie asked Nuisance. "What will you do?" she asked, lifting Nuisance to the floor and stiffly stretching out her legs. "I can't help it," she said, standing up. "I'd really get in trouble, even if I let you stay on the porch."

"Meow," said Nuisance, sorrowfully, hopelessly.

"I can't leave the poor cat outside, not on a bitter night like this. It might freeze to death," she said to herself.

"How *can* I help you?" she said to Nuisance. Cal? Cynthia and Rosalie? Her own real father? At that hour there was no one she could call on.

"Meow!" said Nuisance.

"I'm trying to think of something," said Julie.

"Have you fed the cat?" she remembered Stephen saying. "Not a little bit of milk or something?"

"No one will know," said Julie, feeling very wicked, "if I give you a little bit of milk. Maybe that would keep your blood flowing and keep you from freezing."

"Once you feed a stray cat, it's yours forever," she heard Stephen saying.

"But that's all right," said Julie to Nuisance. "Because that's what I want. For you to never go away, until . . . ." Until what? She wouldn't think about that right now. She got out her key and turned it in the lock. "I'll be right back," she said and slipped into the kitchen before Nuisance could follow her.

Should she heat the milk? she wondered. Even

though her hands were almost numb, she could feel how cold the milk was inside the carton. She wouldn't care to drink warm milk ever, even on a freezing cold night, except in cocoa. But babies liked their bottles warm. Her real father used to tell about warming bottles for her in the middle of the night when she was a baby.

"I thought that bottle'd never get warm," he'd laugh and say. "And there you were crying your head off."

"Why aren't you here to help me warm some milk for Nuisance?" she accused her dad. She felt deserted. No parents, no friends, only . . . . She heard an insistent meow from outside. Only Nuisance.

"I'm coming," she called. "I won't be long." As she went to the cabinet to get a pot for heating the milk, she noticed a sheet of paper on the kitchen table with a phone number written on it.

"They can wait. They can worry," she said to herself.

"*Meow!*" said Nuisance.

"I'm coming," Julie called again. She dipped her finger into the milk to see if it was warm. Was it too warm?

"Then I'd try a little on the back of my hand and it would be too hot and then I'd have to sit and wait for it to cool," her dad would say with a chuckle. "And I'd pick you up. And rock you in my arms."

"And sing me lullabies," Julie would say.

" 'Sleep, baby, sleep. Your father guards the sheep,' " her dad would sing, even when she was big, kissing her on the top of her head.

Julie got a spoon and put a drop of milk on the back of her hand. Did it burn? Did it feel cold?

"Meow!" Nuisance persisted.

"I'm coming! I'm coming!"

After Julie poured the milk in a cracked yellow bowl she found at the back of the kitchen closet, she carried it slowly toward the door so it wouldn't spill. There was no problem about getting through the door quickly. Nuisance knew that Julie had something to eat and followed her so closely that Julie almost tripped. Julie hardly had time to get some newspaper and put the bowl on it before Nuisance was lapping frantically.

"Poor Nuisance," said Julie, kneeling down to watch the cat drink. "How long has it been since you've had any food?" Nuisance did look thinner, and Julie had no trouble feeling ribs under the soft fur. "Poor Nuisance," said Julie again. "You've got to have someone to take care of you."

The telephone started to ring. "I'll be right back," said Julie, but Nuisance was too preoccupied with lapping milk to notice that she was leaving.

"Hello," Julie said. She knew it would be her mother. She didn't reproach Julie for not calling sooner. But she sounded very pleased to hear Julie's voice.

"I didn't wake you, did I, dear?"

"No," said Julie. There was a silence. Julie felt she should explain why she was still up, but she couldn't do it without lying and she felt guilty enough already.

"Well, go to bed soon," her mother said. "We won't be long."

"How long?" Julie asked.

"About half an hour," she said, "but don't wait up for us."

"Okay." Julie hung up.

"Meow!" Nuisance must have finished the milk. Julie poured a little more into the pot and turned up the gas.

"Time for one more round," Julie said as she fetched the bowl, which Nuisance had licked dry. "No, you can't come in," she said when Nuisance tried to squeeze past her into the kitchen. This time she put the second bowl of milk outside the porch door, behind a bush. That'll attract Nuisance away from the porch, she thought. Then I'll get it in the morning before Mom and Stephen are up. Her strategy worked. As she snuck back onto the porch, Julie could faintly see the cat's head bobbing up and down while it drank the milk. Now I know how Hansel and Gretel's parents felt when they had to leave them in the forest to starve, she thought as she closed the porch door securely.

She got ready for bed quickly, listening all the while for the sound of a car in the driveway. Or another sound. The sound of Nuisance asking for more milk, asking to come into the warm house. Suppose Nuisance was waiting at the door when her mom and Stephen got back? Then what? I can't worry about it anymore, Julie decided as she pulled the lifetime quilt up to her chin. Nuisance wasn't in the house so they couldn't complain. And then they'd know that Nuisance really was a stray cat and that something had to be done.

Was that Nuisance she heard? She listened intently. Noises echoed so through the cold night air. A bang and then a thud. Was that Mom and Stephen opening the kitchen door? Or was it robbers trying to get in? Julie lay in bed tensely, waiting for another noise.

"I'll turn the lights out." That was Stephen's voice. What a relief! And he didn't sound upset. His voice sounded deep and strong. Even though it was Stephen's voice, it was reassuring.

Now I can go to sleep, Julie thought. It's so late. It must be after one o'clock. If I opened my eyes, I could look at the clock and see. If I just turned my head and opened my eyes . . . .

She had the feeling that she wasn't sleeping at all. But every time she thought she was wide awake, she found that her eyes were closed and that she was in fact dreaming that she was awake. She kept thinking that she heard Nuisance quite clearly all the way outside at the back door, pleading to be let in out of the cold. Nuisance wants me. Nuisance needs me, she thought.

She looked at the clock, but her eyes wouldn't focus on the time. No, she only dreamed that she looked at the clock. She must force them open to look at the time. Had she really seen it now? Was it 3:34? Then she had been asleep since Mom and Stephen came home. And here she was falling asleep again.

"Wake up! Wake up!" she said to herself. "I simply can't get out of this warm bed," she protested to herself. "You mustn't let an abandoned cat freeze to death," she countered. "But what can I do?" she argued with herself. "You can give it warm milk," an admonishing voice within her responded.

"All right," she said to herself. "All right I'll try."
Oh, it was so hard to wake up. It was so warm under
the covers and so cold in her bedroom. 3:44. Only ten
minutes! It seemed as though she'd been struggling to
wake up for an hour. Speedily into her slippers and
bathrobe. Then the worst would be over.

With a mixture of scolding and persuasion, she got
herself up out of bed and tiptoed downstairs. The
light from the downstairs hall shone into the kitchen
so that she could see to unlock the door. Unreason-
able as it was, Julie half-expected to find Nuisance on
the back porch, waiting for her to come.

"It's not possible," Julie told herself, "because the
porch door is always locked." She closed the kitchen
door and walked across to unlock the porch door. The
cold wasn't as bad as she had thought it would be.
"But that's because I've been in a warm bed," she
reminded herself. "If I'd been outside all night curled
up under a bush . . . ."

She opened the back door, ready to catch Nuisance
up in her arms. There was nothing there. Only cold,
clear moonlit emptiness. "Nuisance," she called
softly. "Nuisance, where are you?" The moon shone
down directly from above. There were no shadows in
which Nuisance might be concealed. Julie looked toward the garage then back toward the depths of the
yard. No cat.

Suddenly, she felt frightened and foolish, like an
abruptly wakened sleepwalker. How had she come to
be alone outside in her bathrobe and slippers? In the
middle of the night? She locked the doors and turned
back into the shadowy house through which she had

come so bravely when she was bent on rescuing Nuisance. Now she was sure she sensed another presence ready to spring out from behind the kitchen door or lurking under the dining room table.

In the hall, where the light was on, she felt safer. Safe enough even to go around into the dark corner by the steps and look out the hall window. This would be her last attempt. If she couldn't see Nuisance anywhere, she would go back to bed feeling satisfied that she had done all she could. She conquered the eerie feeling that someone might sneak up from behind and put his hand over her mouth long enough to stand looking carefully up and down the driveway.

Nuisance must be there somewhere. Otherwise why would that voice have pulled her out of the security of her warm bed into the cold, unfriendly night? Perhaps Nuisance had gone to wait out the night on someone's front porch. Julie knew she couldn't see Cal's porch, but she could see Mrs. Mitchell's porch projecting out from the darkened house. She could see the posts at either end and the faint outline of the door with the white halo of cards pinned up around it. Did she see a cat with white paws? It would be hard to tell.

"I might as well give up," she said to herself. She didn't know why she kept looking out the window. Maybe she was simply too sleepy to go back upstairs. But as she watched, the stillness of the street was interrupted by motion. A car with no lights on was coming slowly down the street and stopping at Mrs. Mitchell's house. After a minute, someone opened the door and got out. Julie could see the inside light flash on and off. There was someone else, a man, still in the car. The glow from the streetlight outlined his head. Yes, and someone had just gotten out. Julie blinked her eyes several times to make sure she was seeing everything clearly.

"I am awake, aren't I?" she asked herself.

The silhouette of the person who had gotten out was tall and hunched. Another man, thought Julie. He stood for a minute. Is he looking around? Then he quickly went up the path and disappeared into the black hollow of the porch. Like a ghost, thought Julie. But the men were real.

And she was awake, she reminded herself once more. And he was probably on the porch trying the windows, trying the door with "Are You Saved?" written above it. "Robbers!" Not in her house, but at Mrs. Mitchell's. "I'm seeing robbers!" Her mouth was dry. Her throat felt tight. "I was only looking for a cat and I'm seeing robbers!"

Julie started to shiver and couldn't stop. Where was the man now? Had he gotten in? Had he gone round to the back? What should she do? Mrs. Mitchell there alone. Not a witch. Just someone old. Who was getting robbed. Who was maybe getting murdered. "Are You Saved?"

Can I save her? Is there time?

"Mom!" Julie was running upstairs. "Mom! Stephen! Robbers!" She was banging on their door. "Mom! Stephen!" Then she opened it. "Even if I do see them lying in bed together," she said to herself, "I must wake them."

"Darling, what is it?" her mother said sleepily.

"Robbers!" said Julie.

"Are you sure? Where?" said her mother, sitting up. All these questions while the tall, hunched man was forcing open a window, sneaking into the kitchen, arming himself with a carving knife.

"Across the street. Come!" She pulled at her mother's arm.

"Oh, you scared me," she said. "I thought you meant here."

"Across the street at Mrs. Mitchell's. She's old. We have to help her!"

"You stay here, I'll go." Stephen was getting out of bed.

"Be careful, darling," said her mother.

"Don't worry. I'm sure it's nothing," he soothed. Would he ever finish putting on his bathrobe? "Julie, I hope this turns out to be a false alarm." He sounded severe and disbelieving.

"Come!" Julie took his hand and pulled him along the hall and down the stairs. "Look!" She pointed out the hall window toward Mrs. Mitchell's house. Her teeth were starting to chatter.

"You have had a fright," said Stephen. His voice sounded more sympathetic now. "Stop shivering, sweetheart, and tell me what you see." He put a bracing, comforting arm around her shoulders.

The car was still parked in front of Mrs. Mitchell's house. "See the man sitting in the front seat?" said Julie. But Stephen couldn't see him. "Look, see his head there, and his coat collar. Now he's leaning forward. See him?"

"No," said Stephen. What could she do? She couldn't ask Stephen to go outside and look in the car.

"Really, I saw it pull up and stop."

"I have to be sure before I call the police."

"What can we do, Stephen? We have to help."

"Go to bed and forget about it. When daylight
comes, these things usually turn out to have been
nothing." Stephen was right. Julie knew how many of
the robbers that she had wakefully heard sneaking
around their apartment when she and her mom were
alone together had vanished with the dawn. But not
this time.

"I saw the car come," Julie insisted. "I saw the man
get out." How could she convince him? She looked
back toward the car hopelessly. Then she saw something bright and flickering.

"Look! Look! Stephen. There's a light in the car."

"My God! You're right," said Stephen. "Someone's
lighting a cigarette."

"And I told you," said Julie, "someone else went up
to the house and I haven't seen him since."

Julie felt that Stephen's arm was gone and heard
him dialing the telephone in the kitchen. A short number. It must be 911, she thought. She saw the large
glow fade and leave behind it a small spot of light that
flitted around like a live creature. She could imagine
the man in the car puffing anxiously on his cigarette.

He's nervous too, Julie guessed. She heard Stephen
giving the address to the police. Do they have signals?
Or doesn't he know any more than we do about what's
going on inside the house? Whether his partner has
found the silver or the jewels, or money hidden in a
coffee pot? Whether Mrs. Mitchell hears him and is
lying stiff with fright in her bed. Whether he's gone

into Mrs. Mitchell's room . . . . Now she felt she really was asleep and dreaming a nightmare.

"I hope they make it." Stephen was beside her again, looking out the window. His voice sounded husky and his hand was cold as it brushed against hers.

"So do I," said Julie.

"Before the car leaves," Stephen continued, "or I'll feel like a damn fool."

The next moment, they saw the headlights of the car flash on and off. Once. Twice. A minute later a black shadow slid from the house down the front walk and into the waiting car. With a jolt, it pulled away from the house, turning its headlights on again as it left.

"I knew it," said Stephen. "It always happens." At that moment another dark car pulled up, and another followed it, while a third with lights on pulled quickly past them both, leaving behind the chill drone of its siren. "They're chasing 'em!" Julie could hear the triumph in Stephen's voice, even though he spoke quietly.

"It's too late," said Julie. Police with flashlights were climbing out of the two cars and surrounding the house. The dark facade was lit up by the nimble beams of light. Meanwhile, the headlights on the two police cars were turned on and the red lights on top started spinning.

"How do they know to leave?" Julie asked.

"Oh, they have their ways. Lookouts. C.B. radios."

"What'll we do now?" They couldn't continue to be nothing more than spectators of all the noiseless commotion that was going on outside.

"Go to bed," said Stephen.

"Bed!" Julie couldn't think of sleeping. Not without knowing whether Mrs. Mitchell was all right. Are you saved? Did the holy magic save you? Like a shepherd he careth . . . .

"Is everything all right?" Mom was calling down from the upstairs hall. "I heard a siren and then it was silent."

"Back into bed right away." Stephen gave Julie's arm a squeeze and pushed her toward the stairs. Why did he have to start sounding like a father instead of a fellow conspirator?

"But Mrs. Mitchell. I have to know." And he was only a stepfather at that.

"The police don't need our help."

"But if she's all right."

"We'll find out in the morning." Then, calling to her mother, Stephen said, "Don't worry, Marjorie. Everything's fine. Julie and I have it all taken care of." Which means, Julie thought, Julie's doing what I tell her to and she doesn't have any say about anything. She wished that she'd never wakened Stephen, that she'd never gotten up, that she'd never seen Nuisance.

Mom tucked her in as though she was a little girl. "Good night, darling." She kissed her on the hair. "Tell me about it in the morning."

Julie turned her head away. Her feelings were so confusing—about Stephen and Nuisance. And someone else. Oh yes, she thought. Wait till I tell Cal.

The Whole Story

Before Julie got to the kitchen for breakfast the next morning, she knew what Mom and Stephen were going to say. They were going to say, "How was the dance?" and, "Why were you up in the middle of the night?" And I'd better have some answers ready, Julie warned herself.

Instead, when Julie opened the door from the hall, her mother was talking on the telephone. At least she was saying, "Yes . . . no . . . of course," while someone else was doing most of the talking. Then Mom said, "Just a minute. She's right here. You can tell her yourself." She put her hand over the receiver and said to Julie, "It's Mrs. Mitchell. She wants to thank you."

Julie didn't want to be thanked. What could she say to Mrs. Mitchell? "How'd she know?" she asked her mother.

"The police told her we called."

"Do I have to?" she asked.

"It would be nice," her mother said. "She's waiting." She handed the receiver to Julie.

"Hello," said Julie. "Are you all right?"

"You see how good God is," said Mrs. Mitchell's rasping voice. She *does* sound like a witch, thought Julie. "Like a shepherd . . . ." Mrs. Mitchell went on to recite what seemed to be a chain of quotations from the cards around the door.

All Julie needed to say was "Yes" and "Uh-huh."

"God called you to save me," Mrs. Mitchell said. Was that what woke her in the middle of the night? Not the tiny voice of Nuisance, but the powerful voice of God?

"Let me know, dahling, if I can ever help you," Mrs. Mitchell was saying. Help me? With what? Julie wondered. How could Mrs. Mitchell ever help with anything? Julie could picture her at the other end of the phone with her cane and her pointy teeth and her eyes like drills. She probably still had the same nightgown on, the one she was wearing when Julie first saw her.

"I'll pray for you in church tomorrow," Mrs. Mitchell was saying, "and your pretty mother." Did she wear her nightgown to church?

"Thank you," said Julie doubtfully. It made her feel strange to be prayed for by anyone, even a nice witch.

"Come over and see me some time," Mrs. Mitchell was saying.

"Thank you," said Julie. As far as the porch, she said to herself, thinking of the musty dimness of the rooms that she had glimpsed from the front door. But not inside the witch's house.

When she hung up, Mom had a stack of pancakes ready.

"Want some?"

"Sure," said Julie, sitting down and reaching for the syrup.

"Steve?"

"Unless Julie wants them all," Stephen said.

"Are you kidding?" Julie looked over at him, but he wasn't smiling.

"How was the dance?" her mother asked, pouring herself some hot coffee. "Coffee, Steve?"

"Thanks."

How was the dance? Here it was, and she'd better answer quickly if she didn't want Mom to start looking concerned. "I survived." That would be an accurate description of the evening. But it would provoke questions so she said, "Fine." There was a silence while her mother and Stephen waited for particulars.

"Well, I'm glad." Mom finally reached over and put her hand on Julie's arm. "Your first dance seems so important."

Was it only her first dance? Julie already felt old in the ways of dances.

"Julie," Stephen cleared his throat.

Here it comes, thought Julie. The other question. How was she going to explain about Nuisance when Stephen had warned her not to feed the cat? And when he was so hostile toward cats?

"Did your being up in the middle of the night have anything to do with . . . the cat?"

Well, that made it easy. "How'd you guess?" Julie asked.

"It wasn't too hard," Stephen said. "It was waiting at the back door this morning. And . . . I found this bowl." He pointed to the cracked yellow bowl on the counter. What had seemed fairly hidden at night was probably pretty obvious in the daylight.

"The cat was there when I got home last night," Julie explained, "and it was so cold I thought some warm milk would keep it from freezing."

"Then it's our cat now," Stephen said.

"You mean . . .?" Was he saying the impossible? Was he saying they could keep it?

"I mean"—Stephen sighed—"it won't leave now. We'll have to do something with it." Of course, that's what he was saying.

"Such as . . . ?" Julie asked.

"I guess it would be out of the question to keep it," Mom said. "Because of the birds." She looked toward Julie. She had heard it, the excitement and hope in Julie's voice.

"Of course," said Julie, to let her mother know that she understood well enough about the birds, and as she said it, she realized how badly she wanted to keep Nuisance. Something soft and warm to hold. Something to keep her company when Mom and Stephen were out. Something to take care of.

"There must be people who would like a nice cat," said her mother.

"A friendly one," said Julie. She got up from the table without even finishing the pool of syrup on her plate. Her head felt stretched, inflated. Probably from not having enough sleep. She went to the window and looked out. No birds at the bird feeder.

"There's always the county," Stephen said behind her. The county. What did that mean? Julie was going to turn and ask when she saw a cat walking up the driveway toward the house with its tail held high. A gray-striped tabby cat with white paws.

"It does seem to think it belongs here," Julie said.

"What?" said Mom.

"Nuisance," said Julie.

"What?" said Mom and Stephen.

"The cat," said Julie. "That's what I named it." And

she hoped it made them feel bad, because it made her feel awful to see the cat out there and know that they would have to send it away.

"Oh, Julie . . . ." She could hear the sympathy in her mother's voice.

"I named it Nuisance because I know that's the way you feel about it," Julie said. And she could have said, "And that's the way you feel about me." When she glanced back at Mom and Stephen, they were silent. But they both looked very sorry, as though they were trying to think of a way to help.

"Meow!" Julie could hear Nuisance at the back door.

"That's the cat," said Julie. "Can I feed it?" she asked. "Until we decide what to do with it?"

No one answered. "Well, I will," she said and started for the hall door. She had the silly feeling that she might start to cry. And she didn't want to cry in front of Mom and Stephen. Then they'd really be concerned and she'd be even more of a nuisance to them.

"Might as well," Mom said as she left.

"I guess so," she heard Stephen agreeing.

She barely managed to get her jacket from the hall closet and the milk from the refrigerator before the tears started running down her cheeks.

"It isn't just you," she said to Nuisance, sniffing as she stood in the brick patio outside the porch door watching a hungry pink tongue lick around the edges of the bowl of milk. "It's me," she said. "It's everything." She rubbed away at the cold tears on her cheeks.

"Isn't it time," said a voice at her elbow, "for the Princess Jewel to reward the royal wizard?"

It was Cal right there beside her in her backyard.

What should she do? As soon as she looked at him,
he'd know she'd been crying. Red eyes, smeared
cheeks. What an impression that would make. Besides,
Julie thought, she might start crying again any minute.

"Don't you call that excellent service?" he demanded. "I think I'll go into the business. Spells gua-
ranteed to work in one week or money cheerfully
refunded." He waited for Julie to answer. What could
she do? She couldn't run inside where Mom and Stephen were. She couldn't talk to Cal because she knew
her voice would sound strange. So she bent over to
stroke Nuisance.

"Princess Jewel," Cal said in majestic tones, "did
you or did you not find the cat named Nuisance waiting on your back porch, as I foretold?"

There was a pause. Then Julie said, "Yes," very
softly.

"Well?" said Cal. "Speak up."

Julie stood straight and looked at him. "I did," she
said and started to cry. Then she ran down the driveway.

"Julie," said Cal, running after her and catching her
by the hood of her jacket. "Julie, stop. It's your
friendly wizard."

Julie was crying in earnest now. She didn't even
know why, because she wasn't that upset about Nuisance. But the crying seemed to have its own momen-
tum. The more she got started crying, the harder it
seemed to stop.

She turned and started walking down the sidewalk
the opposite direction from Mrs. Mitchell's house.
Thank goodness the pocket of her winter jacket had a
tissue in it. Even though it was falling apart, it was

something to blow her nose with. Cal didn't say anything more and they walked along together while Julie got herself under control. At first she felt cold from not having gloves or a scarf. But together the exercise and the sun warmed her. Gradually, she found that she could breathe without the catching feeling that crying brings.

After turning left at the next cross street and walking for another block, she guessed it might be safe to talk. But what explanation could she give? Cal would probably think it was silly of her to get so upset over a stray cat. And he'd be right. Nuisance was the end, not the beginning of the problem.

Then how much should she tell him about herself? She hadn't told anyone, not anyone, not her real father, her grandmother in Boston, certainly not her mother, how she felt about Mom and Stephen. Was she going to start confiding in this kid, this boy whom she hardly knew?

They walked down another block toward the park. The sun glinted from frozen patches of water in the street. The sky was so blue it seemed unreal. Like a *National Geographic* picture.

"What does the county do with animals?" asked Julie. Her voice was still unsteady. Starting with a question seemed safer.

"What do you mean?" asked Cal.

"I mean," said Julie, "when they catch them, or"—how should she put it?—"when they come to pick them up?"

"Oh," said Cal. And she could tell that he understood everything.

They had gotten to the park by then. There was a

creek running through it, with tennis courts on one side of the creek and a playground on the other. It was a little playground with a few swings, a jungle gym, and one seesaw. There were two children in snowsuits on the jungle gym. Otherwise, the playground was empty. Julie stopped and leaned against the steel pole supporting the swings.

"You mean your parents agree that it's a stray cat," Cal said, "and now they want to get rid of it." He didn't ask. He knew.

"Yes," said Julie, feeling it was safe to look at him as she said it. Was it because the brown eyes that were usually so teasing were gentle with concern and interest that she went on?

"At least . . . ." Julie walked over to a swing and sat down. Cal sat down on the swing next to her. "They aren't my parents," she said as she pushed off with both feet.

Cal didn't say anything. He started swinging slowly and sympathetically.

"I mean my mom is. But Stephen isn't." It was so easy when they were swinging back and forth, sometimes together, sometimes in opposite directions, each looking straight ahead, to say whatever she felt like saying. Sometimes, Julie wondered if Cal was listening, or whether he was swinging and daydreaming. But when she was sure he hadn't heard her, he'd say, "Then what happened?" or, "Yeah, that's tough." And she'd go on talking.

She talked about everyone, starting with Mom and Stephen. And Stephen and the birds. And the cat. Talking seemed to get easier and easier until she found herself talking comfortably about her real father. "I don't see him often," she said, "now that he lives on the other side of town."

"You know . . . !" Abruptly, Cal scraped his feet to a stop. "You know . . ." he said, his voice rising at the end in a tone of discovery. "You've never had a chance."

Julie slowed her swing down too. "I don't understand," she said.

"I mean, you've never had any choice," said Cal. "All these things happening to you, and nobody asking you what you wanted."

"I think . . . ." Julie paused. The things she was thinking were hard to say, hard to accept. "I think it didn't make any difference," said Julie. "And . . . I think they were afraid . . . to ask."

"Because, of course, you would have told them not to get divorced," said Cal.

"Yes," said Julie, holding her swing very still. Talking to Cal was like extracting a splinter, ever so painful, but you knew it would only hurt in a healing way once it was out.

"And no one asked me where I wanted to live." Julie was thinking out loud. "Not in so many words. They asked me a lot of questions about what it was like with Mom or Dad. But I could tell they assumed that because I was a girl I'd live with my mother. And I didn't think it mattered a whole lot because Dad lived so close. But now sometimes"—Cal had turned to look at her and Julie looked back—"I wish I lived with my dad."

Was it a cloud over the sun or a shadow on Cal's face? Had Julie said something that disturbed him? "Well, I do," Julie insisted.

"Sure, I understand," said Cal, but he still looked troubled.

"Mom did ask me," Julie continued, "if I minded . . . about Stephen." That had been the rest of the conversation when she was sick and Mom had sat down at the foot of the bed to tell her that she and Stephen planned to get married.

"I think I'd be a better mother to you with Stephen," she had said, "because I'd be happier."

"I did mind," Julie told Cal. "First, it was awful when Dad left and then I got used to it. I even liked being alone with my mother all the time. It was calmer. Now Stephen was going to upset everything again."

"Didn't you say that to your mom?"

"I couldn't," said Julie, "because . . . ."

"Yes?" said Cal.

"Because of something that happened. I can't tell you about it."

"Why not?" Cal's voice sounded tolerant, as though nothing would surprise him.

"It's . . . ." said Julie. "It's too embarrassing. But it was my fault, and my mom decided to marry Stephen right afterward."

"You didn't cause something as big as that. Your mom just did what she wanted."

"You think so?" said Julie, pushing her swing into motion again.

"You couldn't even have caused it if you'd tried to. And you didn't," Cal continued.

"Definitely not," Julie agreed.

"Of course, you can't change what's happened." Cal wrapped his arms around the chains of the swing as though he was drawing his thoughts together.

"No," said Julie, "and I've got Stephen in my life now. Which means getting used to what he likes and doesn't like. Like birds and cats. And it means having the feeling that I'm a nuisance."

"A nuisance?" said Cal. "I thought that was the cat."

"It's me, too," said Julie.

"Why?" asked Cal.

"Because I know Mom and Stephen . . . . I'm sure they want to be alone," said Julie. "I make them uncomfortable. They're always peeking to see if I'm around before they kiss, and . . . ." About the closed door and the double bed? How could she say the rest? Cal waited. "You know about married people," she finished.

She and Cal weren't looking at each other, which made it easier to explain.

"So you feel you're in the way?" he said.

"That's right," said Julie. She was glad he hadn't sniggered about the kissing. Most boys would have.

"Then you should get out of the way," said Cal.

"You mean live with my dad?" asked Julie.

"I mean," said Cal slowly, as though inexorable logic had forced him to it, "be independent. It's your turn to decide what you want and try to make it happen."

"I want a cat," said Julie promptly. "I want to keep Nuisance."

Cal laughed. He seemed relieved. "I'm glad that's it," he said, "and not the other."

"What other?" asked Julie.

"Going to live with your dad."

"But there's no hope," said Julie, "about the cat."

"You're sure? No hope?" said Cal, starting to swing once more.

"None," said Julie, pushing herself back and forth with one foot, trying to stay even with Cal. "Not with birds."

"The county," said Cal. "Sounds bad."

"Like what?" asked Julie.

"Murder," said Cal.

"Cal, you don't mean it." Julie stood up and started shaking his swing. "You're kidding me."

"Hey, stop," said Cal, grabbing her arms as his knees bumped into hers. "I'm not." For an instant, Julie felt the same thrill of intimacy that she had felt when they were sitting on the steps together. Then he dropped his hands and she moved away from him, putting her own hands in her jacket pockets.

"I thought it was like an adoption agency," she said.

"Ask your parents, I mean your mom and Stephen."

"If you're right," Julie said, "that's awful." Her voice shook and she thought she might cry again.

"Come on, Jewel. We'll find a way." Cal stood up and started to move toward her protectively.

"Cal! Cal!" Captain Crunch was shouting from across the creek. "I've been looking everywhere for you."

"Well, here I am," said Cal. He glanced from Captain Crunch back to Julie as though he wished they were still alone. "What is it, child?" he called, walking toward the edge of the creek. Julie followed him. "Why the excitement?"

"Your spell worked," said Captain Crunch, starting to scramble down the bank.

"Which one?" Cal shouted back. "I'm a very busy

wizard," he said to Julie, and the twinkle was back in the brown eyes.

"Don't fall in. The ice is still thin," called Julie as Captain Crunch hurried from stepping stone to stepping stone across the creek.

"Your spell," he said again breathlessly, climbing through the thick grass up the bank on their side. "It worked."

"They always do," said Cal.

"There's a gray-striped tabby cat with white paws sitting on our front porch. It's the friendliest cat. It was climbing all over me," Captain Crunch continued as he pulled himself up to the top of the bank. "But I'm okay," he said, proving it by opening his mouth and breathing deeply and loudly.

Julie felt another pang of affection. Soft, trusting, friendly, bothersome Nuisance. What *did* the county do with cats?

"At least it half-worked," Captain Crunch added, "'cause you said the cat would appear on Julie's porch."

"And where did you first see this cat after the spell was put on it? Answer truthfully, Princess Jewel."

"On our back porch," Julie admitted.

"See," said Cal, patting Captain Crunch vigorously on the head. "You are young yet in the ways of magic, but you will learn to trust your elders who—"

"Cal," Julie interrupted.

"What is it, Jewel?" Something in the tone of her voice made his eyes serious. Captain Crunch slipped out from under his hand and ran over to the playground.

"Have you ever done it?" asked Julie.

"Done what?" said Cal.

"Made up your mind you wanted something, and then made it happen."

Cal looked at her without saying anything.

"Of course, you might not remember," Julie suggested.

"But I do remember," said Cal.

"And did it work?" Julie persisted. "You might not want to, but could you. . . ." Just because Cal knew all about Julie didn't mean he'd want to talk to her about his own feelings.

"Yes?" said Cal.

" 'I'm the king of the castle,' " Captain Crunch called from the top of the jungle gym.

"Could you tell me what it was, Cal?"

"It was," Cal said, "I decided . . . ." It seemed hard for him to express it. Julie was sorry she had asked. "I decided . . . ." Cal was determined to find a way to say it. "That it was time I got to know a girl."

"Oh, Cal!" Julie hadn't expected a revelation like that.

"And so I did," Cal said. "Just one."

Then he waited, as though he wanted some reassurance from her, some indication that she'd understood. Julie tried to put what he'd said together with his reaction to Cynthia and Rosalie and his talk about ninth graders being invisible.

"Then you've told me your secret," said Julie. "The way I've told you mine."

"You guys coming?" called Captain Crunch from the jungle gym.

"Yes," said Cal with a big smile. "It's our secret. And I've got what I wanted," he said, taking Julie's cold hand in his warm one, "except when I get interrupted. I think I know a spell that will make Captain Crunch disappear," he said, leading the way to the jungle gym.

Cal didn't try any of his spells on Captain Crunch after all. Instead he and Julie chased him around the jungle gym.

"I'm a squirrel," he said, sitting up with his hands together as though he were eating a nut. Then he slid down to the ground and ran over to the seesaw. It balanced perfectly when Cal sat on one end and Julie and Captain Crunch sat on the other. When Cal kept them dangling in the air, Captain Crunch would get excited and start screaming, "Let me down, Cal! Let me down."

It was hard to believe that the playful, teasing boy on the other end of the seesaw was the same as the sober boy on the swing, the one who had tried so hard to understand Julie's problems.

Cal's changed my life, Julie thought as they jolted up and down, trying to sort it out while she was holding Captain Crunch and saying "whee!" each time they swung up and Cal swung down.

"The important thing is to decide," Cal said as they were walking home. "It makes you more in control," he said.

Control! That was exactly what Julie needed. More control over her life. You were a nuisance when you were like the cat. Hanging around all the time. Not able to do anything for yourself.

"Go on, Cal," she said. "Go on with the pep talk."

Cal laughed. "Hey, Jewel, aren't your hands cold?" he asked. "Here, take my gloves."

"That's okay," said Julie.

"No," Cal insisted. "They're magic. They'll make all your wishes come true."

Julie scrunched her fists up inside the gloves so the fingers flopped about loosely. It was a personal, intimate feeling to be wearing Cal's gloves. What should she wish? Cal was silent, as though he were giving her a chance to decide. There was no point in wishing things that would never happen, like having her parents together again or having Stephen vaporized. She could wish to live with her father. But that was such a hard, complicated wish. She didn't even know if it was what she really wanted.

"Thought of one?" Cal asked, smiling down at her.

"Getting there," said Julie.

"Don't tell," Cal warned, "or it won't come true."

They turned down Raymond Street. In half a block she'd be home and it would be time to give Cal's gloves back. "I wish," she said to herself, quickly, mindlessly, the way one wishes on birthday candles, "for a home for Nuisance."

"Hope they work," said Cal, taking the gloves back from Julie as they stood at the foot of her driveway. "They did for me."

"Cal, it's lunchtime," Captain Crunch called from across the street. He had run on ahead of them.

"Little brothers!" Cal grimaced. Then he said in a low voice, "Good-bye, Jewel." And left.

Julie lingered to watch Cal swing Captain Crunch up the steps and follow him in the front door of their house.

Then she was alone. Alone where no one can follow

me, Julie thought. Alone in the world of my wish. Why didn't I wish I could keep Nuisance? she asked herself. Isn't that what I really want? No, it was second, she decided. If she was going to succeed, she had better try for something possible, more possible, for example, than having Dad tutor her in math. What she wanted first, and what she had the best chance of getting, was a home for Nuisance.

More in Control

"Ready for lunch?" her mother said. She was opening a can of soup when Julie came into the kitchen. "Is vegetable all right?"

"Sure," said Julie. It wasn't her first favorite. Maybe her third favorite. She liked the alphabet noodles. She could always hope she got the right letters—a C for Cal or an N for Nuisance.

"It'll be hot in a minute," her mother said.

"Thanks," said Julie as she went out into the hall. "Now I know what I want," she repeated to herself as she hung up her jacket. "Now I have to make it happen."

Where to begin? First of all, I need to know if Cal's right about the county, Julie decided. If he is, it's urgent. It's life or death for Nuisance. The only way to find out was to ask.

"Would you get the soup dishes?" her mother said as she came back into the kitchen.

"For three?" said Julie.

"Of course."

Then she'd have to ask in a hurry about the county, unless she wanted to get Stephen involved. Which she didn't.

"Mom,"—she tried to sound casual—"what does the county do with cats?"

186

"Don't tell," Cal had said about her wish, "or it won't come true."

I'm going to be in control, Julie thought to herself. And I'm not going to let other people mess it up.

"I'm not certain," Mom said, "but I think they keep them for a few days and if nobody claims them or wants to adopt them, they . . . put them to sleep."

"Oh," said Julie. She and her mother didn't look at each other. As she was dishing out the soup, Mom said, "Steve only meant that as a last resort."

"Not the way he feels about cats," said Julie.

"It's more the way he feels about birds," said her mother reflectively. She seemed to be answering a question of her own.

In the middle of lunch, at the moment Julie had found both a C and an N in the same spoonful of soup, Stephen, who was facing the window, stood up. "Look! Wait! Don't move. Quiet!" He tiptoed toward the window. Julie stopped her soup spoon halfway up to her mouth. Mom put her glass of water down soundlessly.

"It's a . . . I think it's a . . . ." Julie didn't move. She didn't even turn her head. "That's it, the yellow. A little bit on the wings. And there, on the tail."

Julie could hear the excitement popping in Stephen's voice like soda bubbles, contained inside him for fear of scaring the bird and because he was a contained kind of person.

"It's a pine siskin," he said as though he was seeing a vision. "If you come over very quietly . . . ."

Julie held her breath and so did Mom. They tried to move, without seeming to move, over to the window.

They got there in time to see a little bird, smaller than a sparrow, dart away from the bird feeder.

"Wait a minute," Stephen said, reaching out toward them. "Don't go yet. It'll probably come back."

They waited, leaning over the sink to be as close to the window as possible. The three of them waited and watched. Over toward the garage something was moving. Looking smug enough to have eaten the pine siskin, although there was no way a cat could have caught such a small, quick bird, Nuisance came slowly stalking around the bird feeder.

"Well," said Stephen, going back to his place, "we'd better call the county on Monday." Julie and her mother followed.

"If we don't have a better idea," Mom said as they sat down.

"I wish Julie hadn't fed it," Stephen said, not loudly, but with anger held in, the way he had held in his excitement.

"It was so cold," Julie defended herself. "And I thought it might die."

"I know." Stephen relaxed a little. "But a pine siskin . . ." he almost moaned.

"It'll come back, won't it?" Mom asked. "Now that it knows there's food here."

"I hope so," said Stephen, "once we get rid of the cat."

Get rid of! Despite her mother's assurances that the county was a last resort, it sounded ominous.

I've got to act soon, Julie resolved. If I'm going to stay in control.

A home for Nuisance. Julie kept the goal before her

throughout the afternoon, mulling over strategies for getting to it while she helped her mother with the grocery shopping.

Assuming there's no chance of keeping Nuisance myself, Julie thought as she waited in line with the loaded cart while Mom looked for sunflower seed.

"I still don't know where they put it," Mom confessed.

And obviously there is no chance, Julie continued. Then where would I most like Nuisance to be?

"Decide what you want now and try to make it happen." Julie could hear Cal encouraging her as though he were standing in line behind her, whispering in her ear.

She imagined herself turning around and saying to Cal, "I want you to have Nuisance." She pictured Cal holding the cat, like a shepherd. Where had she gotten that idea? Oh, yes, from Mrs. Mitchell's door.

"Found it," said her mother. She put two big plastic bags with pictures of cardinals on them into the shopping basket. "One wild bird food and one pure sunflower," said her mother. "Stephen mixes his own blend."

"Too bad," said Julie.

"What?" said her mother.

"That birds and cats don't mix."

"I know," said her mother sympathetically. They were next, so they started piling the groceries on the counter. "I wish I could think of a way to make everyone happy," she said.

Mom understands me so well, Julie thought. Even though I've never told her, she knows I'd love to keep the cat. But she's caught between Stephen and me. As her mother opened her pocketbook to get out the money, her hands seemed to shake a little. It'll be helping her, Julie thought, if I take charge and find a home for Nuisance.

Where would I next most like Nuisance to be? The shopping was finished. The groceries were put away and Julie had a few minutes to lie on her couch and look out over the fretted branches to the dim mystery of the twilight sky. Soon Mom would be calling her to get ready because they were going out for pizza. Julie's choice. Definitely pizza over seafood.

The next best home for Nuisance, Julie decided, would be with my real father. If Lindsay has a cat, it means it's okay to have cats there.

She was counting up the advantages—being able to see Nuisance, a reason to visit Dad more often—when her mother knocked on the door.

"We're leaving in about ten minutes," she called.

"I think I've found the answer," Julie said to herself. Distant, not yet grasped, but there like the first star twinkling in the darkness outside.

"Now, I've got to figure out how to make it happen."

Julie turned on the light and stood in front of the mirror brushing her hair till it seemed to vibrate with electricity. That's energy, thought Julie, energy making me fast and clever enough to find a home for Nuisance, to save Nuisance from Stephen and the county.

Throughout dinner, even though they had a long wait for the pizza, Julie felt wide awake and alert, ready for opportunity when it came. And it did. Mom and Stephen decided to go birding on the eastern shore the next day.

"Would you like to come?" Mom asked. She was eating her pizza with a fork. Julie could only nibble hers from the tip. It was very hot, but very delicious. "Steve said it's a good time for seeing the Canada geese."

"And it's supposed to be a nice day," said Stephen.

"But we have to leave early, don't we?" Mom looked toward Stephen.

"By six," said Stephen. "And we'll get back after lunch." He was already halfway into his first piece of pizza. He doesn't even notice how hot it is, Julie thought. It's all birds.

"Well," said Julie, "if it doesn't upset things. . . ." She spoke slowly, because she was thinking of a plan while she was speaking. She was thinking that while Mom and Stephen were gone, she would visit Dad and ask him about Nuisance. "I don't really want to get up that early," she said.

"Would you mind very much," Mom said, "if we went without you?"

"Want some more pizza?" Stephen asked.

"Yes, thank you," said Julie, holding out her plate. "Not at all," she said to Mom. "I'll probably be asleep most of the time you're away." As she heard herself saying that she knew she wasn't going to tell her mother about her plan.

It might not work, she reasoned, so why get Mom and Stephen involved. Besides, when they lived in Virginia, she used to visit Dad whenever she felt like it.

If her mother wasn't home, she left a note. All the same, she felt calculating. But I have to be, she reasoned, because of Nuisance. "Don't tell, or it won't come true," Cal had said about her wish.

She telephoned her father that night, secretly in Mom and Stephen's bedroom while they were downstairs watching TV. There was no answer. Suppose he was away for the whole weekend? Didn't he say he was going away the previous weekend? He's probably out on a date, Julie decided. I'll try again in the morning.

She went to bed early. She was exhausted from being up late the night before and up again in the middle of the night. But she didn't go to sleep right away. If Dad isn't there, then what? she kept thinking. So much had happened since the night before. The dance, the robbery, her talk with Cal. How could she go to sleep when there was so much to remember. Cal. She imagined the dance all over again with Cal there dancing with her instead of Arnold Finch.

She heard Mom and Stephen come upstairs and get ready for bed. I'll never sleep, she fumed. I'll still be awake when they leave tomorrow morning. Maybe the robbers'll break in here tonight, she thought. And climb into my room from the porch roof. Julie considered getting up and locking her window.

"Good night, dear," her mom called from outside her door.

How did she know I was still awake? I won't bother about the window, Julie thought, and fell asleep.

After all, she never heard Mom and Stephen leave. And when she woke the next morning, it was ten o'-clock. Late enough to call her father without fear of disturbing him.

"Great idea," he said when she called. "Shall I meet you at the metro? But I can't drive you back, monkey."

"That's okay," said Julie, "I'll go the way I came."

"It's okay with your mom?" he asked.

"Yes," said Julie. Well, Julie was sure it would be, if she knew. Hadn't she told Julie that later, when she visited her father, she could take the R3 bus as well as the metro? "Don't speak to strangers." That's what Mom had said afterward.

"It's okay," she told her father, "as long as I don't speak to strangers." She laughed, and so did he.

"Look," he said, "think you can walk up Connecticut to my apartment? It's only four blocks. Since I won't know exactly when to meet you."

"Sure," said Julie. "I remember where it is."

"And don't forget, it's apartment 808. I'll see you when you get here."

Perfect, Julie thought as she put down the telephone. It's all worked out perfectly. She hurried through dressing and eating breakfast. She wanted to get away before Mom and Stephen returned.

"Have gone to visit my dad," she wrote on a piece of scrap paper. "I'll be back this afternoon." She put the note on the kitchen table.

"Meow, meow." Oh, Nuisance! The sound was close. Right outside the back door. She didn't have time. But of course the cat must be fed. The yellow bowl was in the dish drainer. Julie filled it with milk—no time to heat it—and took it outside. She put it right by the door. Why hide it? Stephen couldn't complain, when Nuisance would soon be gone.

"You'll have a home soon," Julie promised Nuisance. "And then you'll have cat food and cat candy."

She left Nuisance lapping and ran to get her coat. It was sunny again and a little warmer, but still a day for scarf and mittens. When she got back, the bowl was empty. "All right, one more round." Julie poured in such a hurry that the milk slopped out of the bowl onto the bricks.

"Good-bye, Nuisance," she said as she left. "I'm doing this for you."

Good-bye, Cal, she called over, not aloud. This is all because of you.

Good-bye, Mrs. Mitchell, she sent thought waves as she passed the gray frame house. Eleven o'clock. She's probably in church. I hope you do pray for me, Julie was surprised to find herself thinking.

She waited for the bus a long time, wondering if she had the right place. Then a woman with a little boy about the same age as Captain Crunch came and stood and soon after a bus arrived.

Julie gave the bus driver a dollar. "Exact change," he growled.

"Oh, dear," said Julie. Taking the bus without Mom to pay the fare was more complicated than she'd expected.

"I have change," said the woman who was right behind her. She got four quarters out of her open coin purse. "It's fifty cents," she said. "You put it in there." Julie dropped two quarters in a clear plastic tube, where they spun around and disappeared. Then she gave the woman her dollar.

I should have asked whether this went to Takoma, she thought after she sat down. But Mom had told her this was the bus. She hated to go back and ask. When they stopped at the plaza, several people got on and a young man asked, "Is this the bus to the metro?" The bus driver muttered an answer that Julie couldn't hear.

"What?" said the young man.

"Yes, it is," said the woman with the little boy. After that, Julie leaned back and started to enjoy being independent and in control.

She was glad she'd had practice with the metro. There were so many mechanical things that had to be done right. The dollar bill the right way. The fare card the right way. Because it was Sunday morning, there were not many people riding. The train breezed through each station with only the briefest pause. Since she knew that she got off at the end of the line, Julie didn't follow the stops with much attention. It seemed as though she'd only been on the train a few minutes when it stopped emphatically, the last few people in her car stood up, and the sign in the lighted arch of the station said VAN NESS.

When Julie got to the top of the escalator, she looked up and down Connecticut Avenue and started off the opposite way from the zoo. She passed a drugstore, a laundromat, and a shoe store. Then she had to stop for a red light. Should she bring Nuisance by bus and metro, she deliberated as she waited for the light to change, or would it be best if her father came and took Nuisance back in his car?

Of course I'd go along and keep Nuisance from climbing all over the place. I wonder if Nuisance has ever ridden in a car? Julie looked ahead of her as she continued up Connecticut. This was the second block.

Two more to go. It seemed much colder and windier than it had at home. The wind was coming straight at her. She leaned into it as she walked along.

Her dad was right. Four blocks to the apartment building. There was no doubt about the circular drive. As Julie opened the heavy glass door, the warm air rushed out and sucked her in. She stood for a moment on the red carpet, trying to orient herself. What was she looking for? The elevator, of course. Being in an apartment building seemed familiar, as though she'd never left Virginia. The door opened and Julie stepped out into the hall. The hall smelled like an apartment house. The odors of different breakfasts still lingered—bacon mixed with coffee mixed with sausage mixed with toast.

808. Julie rang the bell and waited. No answer. She rang again, holding the bell longer this time. Still no answer. She put her ear to the door to see if she could hear it ringing. Yes, she could. What had happened to Dad? Maybe he had gone back to sleep. With her right hand she rang the bell and with her left she knocked as hard as she could. Someone down the hall opened a door and looked out. So Julie stopped knocking. And she stopped ringing too. It was clear that no one was going to answer.

She leaned against the door. She felt dizzy from the hot air in the hall after the cold air outside. And from ringing. And from disappointment. What should she do? Go back, of course. The elevator. The walk. The metro. The bus. It was such a long trip. She might as well be going around the world. And alone. That was the worst part. The empty feeling of being alone.

Julie went slowly back along the hall to the elevator and pushed the "down" button. The elevator was coming from below. Julie watched the lights that traced its ascent. It stopped. The doors opened and someone got out. It was Dad. He was holding the Sunday paper.

"Hello, monkey," he said, leaning around the paper to kiss her on the cheek. "Been waiting long? You got here sooner than I expected."

"That's okay," said Julie. It seemed okay now that he was walking back down the hall with her.

"I hope you won't be shocked," he said as they stood at the door of 808 and he felt in his pocket for the key. "I haven't made my bed yet."

After the dark hall, it was a surprise to step into the sunny apartment, like the difference between having Dad not there and then there.

"It's pretty well fixed up," he said, putting the paper on the couch. "Lindsay helped me hang the pictures." For Julie, the pictures were old friends—the painting of the ocean, the enlarged photograph of her dad's sailboat, *The Turnabout.* And there was a picture of her, this year's school picture in its cardboard frame, on the table by the couch. It made Julie feel sad to think of Dad having her picture for company instead of having her.

"Had breakfast?" he asked.

"Before I left," said Julie.

"What about lunch?"

"Isn't it early?"

"I know," he said. "We'll have brunch."

They had bacon and eggs and honey buns from the

bakery down the street. "Want some coffee?" asked her father.

"A little," said Julie. Mom would have a fit. "Where's the brunch part?"

"Well," said her father, "we could have ice cream. Or tuna fish."

They ate at a little wooden table in front of the bay window. Julie could look out and down while they ate and see the cars and buses on Connecticut Avenue.

"What's on your mind?" he asked while they were sipping coffee. Julie's had lots of milk and sugar in it.

How was it, she wondered, that parents were always intuiting things before you were ready to tell them?

"What about your math?" he asked.

"Oh, that's all worked out," Julie said.

"Good! Anything else?" No point in keeping him guessing.

"Yes," said Julie. "It's a stray cat. I wondered if you'd like to have it."

"And you came all this distance," he said, going over to the coffee table to get his pipe and tobacco, "to bring me and a stray cat together."

"Yes," said Julie, "I came because I want to find a home for it. And I'd most like to have it living with you." With Nuisance's fate hanging in the balance, her father scooped tobacco into his pipe and packed it down with his finger.

"Forgive me," he said, striking a match and holding it above the bowl of the pipe, "if I (puff) ask (puff) an obvious (puff) question. But why (a big puff and a marvelous, pungent aroma) can't the cat live with you?"

"Because . . . ." Julie always had the feeling that Dad

didn't want to hear about Stephen, that he didn't want
to accept the fact that her mother had remarried. "His
problem is, he never faces reality," her mother always
claimed.

Well, it was easy enough for him to pretend. He
didn't have to see Stephen every day. But it wasn't fair
for Julie to bear the burden of adjusting to Stephen
alone. Now he had to help her. He was sitting back in
his chair with his legs crossed, cradling the bowl of the
pipe in his hand while he puffed, waiting for her to
continue.

"Stephen likes birds," she said, "and he hates cats."

"I see," said her father, emitting a leisurely aura of
smoke. "That's a problem. There are cat lovers in this
world and bird lovers and it's hard for them to find a
meeting place."

"And there're people in the middle," said Julie.
"That's me. I like both. But this cat. It's very friendly.
And Stephen's talking about calling the county."

"It must be . . . . Want some more coffee?"

"No, thanks," said Julie. She was having trouble
finishing her first cup.

"It must be an outdoor cat," he continued, "not an
apartment cat. Even if it were, monkey, I'll tell you
honestly, I don't have the time. And "—he took his
pipe out of his mouth and leaned toward her—"it
would be no substitute for having you."

"Oh, Dad," said Julie. She wanted to run around the
table and sit on his lap and put her head against his
shoulder, but she was too big for that. Instead, she
looked out the window. "I wish I could live with you,"
she said, not looking at her dad.

"I understand," he said very softly. Julie could smell

his pipe and hear the quiet hiss of his puffing. "Stephen's still new on the job," he said. "Give him a chance. He'll work into it all right."

He stood up and paced down to the other end of the living room without saying anything more. Julie knew that he was thinking about all the old hurts: the separation, the divorce, and then her mom marrying again.

But what about her? She was trying to make something happen her way for a change. She started clearing off the dishes with the numb feeling that when it came to finding a home for Nuisance, she was right back where she had started.

The Rescue

They stayed in the apartment and watched the basketball game on TV until it was time for Dad to pick up Lindsay. "We're going to a concert," he explained. "That's why I can't take you home. But we'll drop you off at the metro."

"Julie!" said Lindsay when she came to the door. "Are you coming with us?" Dad seemed pleased at the suggestion.

"Would you like to?" he asked Julie.

"No, I've got to get home," said Julie. She wasn't interested in concerts. And it was after four. And she wanted to get back to her mother. She wanted very badly to get back to her mother.

They sat the same way in her father's car. With Julie in the middle. "Julie's trying to find a home for a stray cat," he said as they drove along. Was he hoping that Lindsay would be interested, or was he making conversation? Why not Lindsay? As long as Dad kept seeing Lindsay, Julie would be able to see Nuisance. But if Lindsay eventually disappeared, like all of her dad's other girl friends . . . . Julie wasn't sure she should take a chance on losing Nuisance to Lindsay.

"Aren't you wonderful!" Lindsay put her arm around Julie and gave her a squeeze. "If Genghis Khan—that's my cat—didn't think it was his duty to exterminate all other cats, I'd take it for you." Then, when it was obviously impossible, Julie knew that she would have been glad for Nuisance to live with Lindsay.

Right before the metro, Dad turned the corner so Julie wouldn't have to cross the street to reach the entrance.

"You know how to do it?" he said.

"Of course," said Julie. "I made it this far, didn't I?"

Lindsay had gotten out of the car and was waiting, holding the door open. "I wish you luck with the cat," she said. Her voice had the lilt of a good fairy's promise.

"Maybe next weekend," said Dad, kissing Julie on the cheek. "I'll call you."

Maybe not, thought Julie. With the long return trip ahead of her, she had no interest in coming back again next weekend, without Nuisance.

As she rode down the escalator, Julie still saw the images of her dad and Lindsay in her yellow cloak next to him waving to her as she left. "He'll probably marry her," she said to herself calmly as the escalator carried her from daylight to darkness. Then she'd feel cut off from her father the way she felt cut off from her mother. At least Lindsay seemed glad to see her, whereas Stephen . . . she wasn't sure.

Although she'd taken the metro from Takoma to Van Ness twice, this was the first time Julie had made the return trip. Of course, the first part was easy for her, getting a new fare card and going through the turnstile. But then she had to decide where to wait. I've really got to concentrate, she thought as she studied the arrows pointing toward the trains. She followed the Silver Spring arrow down some stairs onto a platform. Hope this is right, she thought. I could ask. She looked around at the people who were waiting. "Don't speak to strangers," she heard Mom saying. She promptly looked down at her feet.

If other people are waiting here, then the other side's the end of the line, and this must be the right side, she reasoned and felt reassured. She looked up again, way up, at the dimly lit arch of the subway station. Cautiously, she looked around her at the shadowy figures scattered along the platform. It was a little bit eerie. Not like waiting in the daylight at Takoma. She'd be glad when the train came. The recessed lights at the edge of the platform began to blink. "Get ready. Get ready," they blinked. Then Julie heard a roaring sound coming closer and saw a small light like a Cyclops eye getting larger and larger as it sped toward her out of the dark tunnel. Before she had time to read the name as carefully as she would like, the train whizzed past her and stopped. Frantically, she reconstructed the glimpse she had had of a lighted panel in front. It read, she was sure it read SILVER SPRING.

"And I get off at Takoma," she recited to herself as she sat down by a window. Where was the map of the metro stations? She'd need it this time, since she wasn't getting off at the end of the line. She looked around and saw one on the wall beyond her seat. By leaning over the seat in front, she could see the map and the names of the stops written on it. Van Ness. That's where she started, then . . . how many stops had

the train gone through already? One or two? Good
heavens! She had lost track. But they couldn't be near
Takoma yet. They had to come out from underground
first. She watched carefully for the name of the next
stop. Metro Center. Now she knew where she was. She
should stop worrying. Nothing was going to go wrong.
Soon she'd be getting off the bus and walking down
Raymond Street. Soon she'd be walking in the back
door and saying, "Hi Mom."

A number of people got on at Metro Center. Julie
could see from the map that it was where the blue line
crossed the red line. Since there were lots of extra
seats, even seats by windows, Julie thought it was
strange when a man sat down beside her. There was
even a completely empty seat right in front of her,
nearer the map, and one right behind her. Then why
sit next to her? She tried not to notice him. She kept
looking out of the window even though all she could
see was blackness. Was that the way it was in outer
space? she wondered. You looked out of the window
and you didn't seem to be anywhere. You didn't even
know where you were in relation to time, whether you
were in the past or the future. Time was so mixed up
in outer space. But you knew you were going from
something to something.

She felt the man next to her shift in his seat and
cross his legs. He seemed uncomfortably close to her.
He didn't smell spicy like her dad, but the way Mary
sometimes smelled, as though she'd taken a bath in
cheap perfume. She looked covertly over toward him.
Not up at him, just over. His foot swung into her line
of vision. It had a black, very polished shoe on it. And

she could tell that he was wearing maroon slacks.

She thought he knew she was looking at him so she turned back toward the window. They were pulling into a station, Judiciary Square. She'd missed Gallery Place. How had that happened? She really must concentrate or she'd miss her stop. Blackness again. What had she been thinking about? About coming from and going to. From Dad and Lindsay to Mom and Stephen, back and forth, and not making any progress, not being able to get out of the past into the future. Her own future, a future that she created for herself, rather than one they created for her. Blackness outside. Outer space. Then ahead the faint light of the next stop. It was just as the train was pulling into Union Station and she was leaning forward to look at the map that the man next to her spoke.

"You going far, girlie?" Girlie! It took her by surprise and she looked right at him. He was smiling and she could see his gold tooth and his graying, thin little mustache, which made his lips look red. And his thin, graying hair and his maroon tie to match his trousers. She saw it all while she was trying to decide what to do.

"Don't speak to strangers." How could she avoid it? She could push past him and get off. Then what? Could she get off without paying and wait to take another train? But she might have to wait a long time and anyhow the doors were closing and anyhow, simply because he asked her one question.

"You know where you get off?" he asked. Julie couldn't go on not answering him.

"Yes," she said, and looked back out of the window. At last, daylight! After the blackness it seemed very

bright, even though it was a late winter afternoon
light. They went through the train yards where she
could see a silver passenger train waiting to speed off
to New York or Boston. Beyond it, an endless freight
train toiled its way south. While she was still counting
cars, the metro line diverged from the railroad yards.
Now they were up above everything on the high trestle
that made Julie feel as though she was going to fall
over the edge.

"If you tell me where you're supposed to get off,
girlie, I'll tell you when."

"That's all right. I know," said Julie as chillingly as
possible. "Don't speak to strangers." But what could
she do? She had to shut him up. There were empty
seats. She could move. If only it didn't seem so awkward to push past the maroon slacks and the shiny
black shoes.

RHODE ISLAND AVENUE. Far below the metro tracks
she could see the vast parking lot with a Sunday sprinkling of cars in it. How many stops till Takoma? If she
looked at the map, the man might start talking to her
again. Maybe she'd be lucky. Maybe he'd get off first.
It wasn't much further. She thought she remembered
three stops, four stops after Union Station? Oh, it was
all so lovely—the panorama of the city under the sun-
set glow of the sky with a light coming on here and
there. All spoiled by this provoking man. The train
was stopping again. Brookland. "Get off, get off," she
said to him, but not out loud. He didn't get off. Maybe
at the next stop. The train hardly started up again
before it was slowing down. Was this Takoma? Did it
come after Brookland? She decided she'd stand up
and be ready to get off in case it was.

Was it her imagination, or did the man make it difficult for her to get past him? She almost tripped over one of his shiny black shoes. As she waited, holding onto the pole near the door, she could feel him watching her. With a jerk, the train slowed down. She bent over to see the name of the station. FORT TOTTEN. Not yet. The man didn't get off either.

Now Julie was truly worried. As best she could remember, there were only two stops left—Takoma and Silver Spring. And what if he got off at Takoma? I'll have to pretend he doesn't exist, Julie decided. I'll have to go where I have to go to get the bus and never look back. And if he was the only other person who got off? She'd cope with it if she had to. There were a number of people on the train who still had to get off at one of the next two stops. But it didn't look as though it would still be daylight when she was waiting for the bus. She was later than she had planned to be. The sky was only the slightest bit red now, and most of the cars she saw on the streets below had their lights on.

The train was slowing down again. Julie bent over to read the first sign. TAKOMA! With a final twitch, the train stopped. There was a breathless moment while she waited for the doors to open. Did she hear someone standing up? She didn't look back. "Here goes nothing," she said to herself as the doors opened, and she got off the train.

There was someone getting off behind her, but she didn't look back. At least there were other people getting off from other doors. If that was the man behind her, at least she was not alone. Thank goodness for that! There was even a cluster of people waiting to get onto the escalator. Thank goodness! Thank goodness! Even if he was there behind her, she would not be alone with him. As she went down on the escalator, Julie felt in her pocket for the fare card. She didn't want to hesitate in a way that might invite an offer of help. She wanted to get out of the station as quickly as possible.

She made sure she put the fare card in the right way on the first try. People were going through the turnstile next to her. She was afraid to look, but she did. They weren't? It wasn't? No, she didn't see the man. But when she stood under the streetlight at the bus stop for the R3, and all of the other passengers except for a woman with bleached hair and spike heels seemed to have melted away to other buses or parked cars, she knew he was behind her, watching her.

"He's there, he's there. I can feel it. I know he's there. You don't need to look," she said to herself. But she did look, and he was there in the shadows, sitting on the low wall that ran along the station embankment. And she could tell, even though it was almost dark, that he smiled at her.

"He's following me." She commenced an agitated inner dialogue. "What makes you think so? He just happened to be getting off at Takoma." "He's interested in me. He smiled at me." "It was only a fatherly smile. He probably has five daughters and five sons at home, ages one to twenty. No need to worry."

Julie didn't believe herself and moved closer to the woman with the spike heels. You're wrong, she told herself. I'd better do something, because it looks as though he's waiting for the same bus. And I have to get off and walk home in the dark. And most likely no one will get off at my stop except me and that man.

"He'll turn out to be one of the neighbors you haven't yet met," the comforting voice tried, but Julie ignored it. "How did I get into this situation?" Was there a bus coming? Even if there was, she was still in trouble. She'd wanted to be in control of her life. And she still did. She still meant to find a home for Nuisance. She knew she could manage, if it weren't for the dark. Awful things happen in the dark, she thought as she remembered the hunched man in the dark moonlight trying to break into Mrs. Mitchell's house. The dark was what made her feel helpless.

"Who will care if I never come back?" she asked herself. Her mother would. Julie thought of her mother looking out the hall window into the night, watching for her to walk down the street. And I didn't even say good-bye to you, Mom, Julie mourned. I snuck away while you were gone without ever saying good-bye. But would Mom care as much as she used to, now that she had Stephen? And wouldn't Stephen be glad to have Mom all to himself? He'd be rid of us both, then. Me and Nuisance. After all, Stephen fell in love with my mom and not with me. Maybe no one would care anymore whether she came back.

Lights moving toward them. Was it a bus? If it was the right one, should she take it, even if he took it, and hope again that the man would get off first? Or should she get off with the woman with the bleached hair. And then what? The bus stopped at the plaza. She could get off there and phone. The plaza would be well lit. And there were always a lot of people around.

No, it wasn't a bus. It was a car. Suppose it was someone coming for the woman with the bleached hair! The car slowed down and stopped right in front of where she and the woman were standing. She could see a hand beckoning from the shadows within. And her heart stopped beating. That was it. She was going to be left alone with him. But the woman didn't move. Someone opened the door of the car and called, "Julie." The voice was Stephen's. Of course, and the car was Stephen's. "Stephen, oh, Stephen!" Julie ran to the car and got in. Then, forgetting that he was her stepfather, not her real father, she threw her arms around him and hugged him. "Oh, Stephen, I'm so glad to see you!"

"We didn't want you traveling home in the dark," he said. He hugged her back and held her for a moment. Julie felt safe. Altogether safe. "Close the door, sweetheart," he said. His voice sounded husky and gentle, the way it had the night of the robbery. After banging the door shut as hard as she could, Julie pushed the button down to lock it. Now she could look, and it didn't matter, at the woman standing near the curb and the man sitting away from the light on the wall.

When she looked at Stephen, he was smiling at her as though he was pleased and relieved to see her. "We were worried about you," he said as he put the car in gear. "It gets dark faster than one expects."

"Where's Mom?" Julie asked.

"Getting dinner," Stephen said. Dinner! Home! Light! She had thought she'd never get there.

"How'd you know when to come?" she asked.

"Your dad called to say you were on your way. So I took a chance."

And she was wondering if anyone cared. When they

were telephoning each other, sending urgent messages back and forth. "Where's Julie. Is she safe?"

"No, she needs you. She needs help."

"Then I'll find her, wherever she is. I'll find Julie and rescue her."

"It's lucky your bus didn't come before I did," Stephen said.

"Is it ever!" Julie said. Is it ever, she said to herself about ten times. But maybe it was all quite innocent. Now that she was safe, she wondered if she might have misunderstood.

"How was the trip?" Stephen asked. And Julie told him about it, in particular about the man on the metro. She couldn't believe herself. Here she was talking to Stephen the way she talked to her real father.

If Stephen thought she'd been wrong to go by herself on the metro, he didn't say so. Julie was glad of that. From the security of the car, she could allow herself the pleasing feeling of independence that comes from being able to travel alone.

"He was probably trying to be helpful," said Stephen, "but you can't be too careful."

"Then, if you hadn't come, what should I have done?" Julie asked.

"The plaza was a good idea," Stephen said as they pulled into the driveway. "I'll be glad to come for you, if you need me, wherever you are."

He turned off the engine, but he didn't get out of the car immediately. "By the way," he said, "the cat was there when we got home. So I gave it some milk."

"Oh," said Julie. "Thank you, Stephen." Had he changed his mind about Nuisance?

"But we've got to do something about it." It didn't

sound as though he had. "Some time soon." When was that? How much time did she still have to find a home for Nuisance?

Stephen got out of the car on his side and Julie got out on hers. "Your mom'll be glad to see you," he called across to her. "She'll be glad you're home safely. And the boy across the street," Stephen said at the door to the porch, "wanted to know where you were and when you were coming back. He followed the cat up the driveway."

Cal! Had been openly looking for her! Why did she think she wanted to live with her father, when there were so many people waiting for her at home?

As soon as Julie opened the porch door, Mom opened the kitchen door for her. "Oh, Julie," Mom said, holding her tightly. "You did give us a scare."

"Didn't you find my note?" asked Julie.

"Yes, dear, but it got dark so early."

After dinner, Julie helped clear up and then left to do her homework. At the door she turned back to look around the kitchen. It had never seemed as bright and warm as it did at that moment. And Mom had never looked more beautiful than she did then, standing at the sink to scour the last pot, wearing a little red-polka-dot apron.

"That was a great dinner, Mom," said Julie.

"I know you like fried chicken," she said, turning halfway so that she still held her soapy hands over the sink. "By the way, dear, she said, "I did want to mention . . . we've got to do something about that cat. Some time soon."

Like a Shepherd

"I'll find a home for Nuisance," Julie declared to herself as she was dressing for school the next morning, "before dinnertime tonight." She set that as her deadline because that was when Mom and Stephen were likely to start making other plans for Nuisance, plans that might feature the county. So she wanted to have everything arranged by then. She wanted to surprise them by managing it herself.

During the walk to school, it was hard to find time to ask Cynthia and Rosalie. Although they had already gotten together over the weekend to relive the dance, they wanted to do it again. And they wanted to hear all about Julie's experiences.

"I danced with Arnold Finch, too," said Cynthia. "Wow! Dancing with a math genius! I couldn't concentrate on what I was doing. I kept seeing x's and y's in front of my eyes."

When they were a block away from school, Julie had to choose. Should she tell about the robbery, or ask about Nuisance? Clearly the robbery could wait, while Nuisance needed a home before dinnertime. "You know the cat that's always around our place. Would you like it?" she asked. "Either of you? It's very friendly and it needs a home."

"I'd love to help you out, honey," said Cynthia,

"but my little sister has a canary, and cats and canaries . . . ."

"And we have a dog," said Rosalie. They were turning up the path to the school. A dog, and a canary. Both good reasons for not taking in a stray cat.

"See you this afternoon," said Julie as she left them at the door. Who else might want a cat?

"Poor thing. I'd love to," said Mary when she asked her. "But we already have three. If I brought another one home, my parents might start to notice and kick them all out." Although Julie was disappointed, she felt she understood Mary better. She could imagine that Mary collected boys in the same kindly way she collected cats. She could believe that Mary really had meant to do a nice thing when she shared Scott with her at the dance.

Who else might like a cat? Julie sat at the lunch table after everyone had left, contemplatively munching on a bag of Fritos. She considered Mrs. Barker. She'd been very encouraging to Julie in the hall that morning.

"How's everything going?" she had paused for a moment to ask. "Mr. Hawkins tells me your math has improved."

"I feel as though I understand it now," said Julie.

"Keep up the good work," said Mrs. Barker and left, just as Julie was saying to herself, "Why not ask?" But it really isn't part of her job, thought Julie. She was down to the last five Fritos.

"Has it come true?" someone said, a boy's voice from behind her.

"What?" Julie turned around. Who was it? It sounded like . . . .

"Has your wish come true?" It *was* Cal. He sat down next to Julie.

"I've decided to give up being invisible," he said, helping himself to a Frito. "You don't mind?"

"Have the rest," said Julie.

"Thanks." Cal took the last two. "It's only a matter of being teased," he said. "If you don't care, I don't."

"I don't," said Julie. She thought she must be blushing. It was so unexpected to have Cal sit down by her. Was anybody noticing?

"Besides," said Cal. "I don't get enough chance to talk with you." The bell for classes rang. Cal pushed out his chair. "I can't be late for biology," he said.

"Of course not," said Julie. But she didn't want him to go. There was so much she wanted to tell him. She hadn't even told him about the robbery.

"Can you walk home with me at the end of school?" he asked.

"Sure," said Julie. "Where's your bike?"

"I didn't bring it. See you at the front door." He snatched his books from the table and left.

All Julie wanted to do the rest of the day was think about Cal and how he had given up being invisible at school. How he had even planned it ahead, coming to school without his bike so he could walk home with her. It was easy to dream about Cal during history while Mrs. Allbright was summarizing the causes of the Civil War. But during the tutoring session she had to think about math, because Arnold Finch kept asking questions. And Julie was usually the only one who could answer them. Wilma was too shy and Cynthia was too confused.

At the end of the period, after Arnold and Wilma

had left, Julie hurriedly told Cynthia. "I won't be coming home with you this afternoon."

"Why not?" Cynthia asked.

"I'm walking back with Cal."

"Well, honey," said Cynthia, "you are making progress. Forget about that cat and have fun with Cal."

For an instant, Julie thought that maybe she would forget about the cat. And let it be taken away by the county? And give up trying to make her wish happen? It was only an instant.

"I meant to tell you that I gave the cat some tuna fish," said Cal as they were waiting to cross East-West Highway. Julie thought she might feel awkward walking back from school with Cal, but they had so much to talk about that it seemed as comfortable as all the other times she'd been with him.

"When?" said Julie.

"Last night," said Cal. And milk from Stephen. For one night at least, Nuisance had been well fed. "My mom said it was okay, temporarily. Have you got your wish?" He repeated his question.

"Not yet," said Julie. "And I'd better get it soon, because I don't have much time left. And I don't know how I'm going to do what you said. Make it happen."

"You could try wearing my gloves again, if you think that would help."

"Thanks!" Julie laughed. "I think I need something stronger."

"What about a witch," Cal suggested. They were passing Mrs. Mitchell's house.

What about Mrs. Mitchell? "Let me know, dahling, if I can ever help you." Julie looked toward her door.

By its shape, she could tell that the card with the picture of the shepherd holding a lamb was still there.

Like a Shepherd He Careth for Thee.

In her imagination, she tried to replace the picture of the shepherd with the image of Mrs. Mitchell holding Nuisance in her arms. Was it possible? How would it work? How would she hold a squirming cat when she had to lean on her cane? Maybe, she thought, maybe I'll ask her. But the door looked very closed and forbidding.

While Julie helped Cal to assemble the newspapers, she told him about the robbery.

"I heard it, I know I did," said Captain Crunch, who was helping too. "I woke up in the middle of the night and I heard squeaks and rattles."

"That was in our house, not Mrs. Mitchell's house," said Cal.

"Maybe they came to our house first," insisted Captain Crunch.

Cal looked toward Julie with a what-can-you-do expression. "At least they didn't take anything. Right, Crunch?"

"I haven't been able to find my Super Ball," said Captain Crunch.

"I give up," said Cal. He started loading his papers onto his bike.

"Ask her, Jewel," he said before he left. "I'll bet witches have a way with wishes. See you later."

Julie watched Cal on his bike until he turned the corner at the end of the block. She was sorry he'd left.

It was a perfect day for sitting and talking, even out-side. Almost like spring again. A day for crocuses and early robins.

I'll take his advice, she decided, and go ask Mrs. Mitchell. As she was still standing in front of Cal's house, nerving herself to ring Mrs. Mitchell's door-bell, the door opened and Mrs. Mitchell came out. She was holding a broom and had her cane hanging over her arm. She came down the steps, leaning heavily on the railing, and started sweeping the path.

She must be a witch, thought Julie. Do I dare ask? she debated. The behavior of witches was unpredict-able. But witches can do things that ordinary humans can't, like saving stray cats. So I must be brave.

"I'm going to try," she told Captain Crunch. "Wanna come along?"

"Not me," said Captain Crunch. "I don't want to be turned into gingerbread."

"Tell Cal if I'm not in school tomorrow to look for me in Mrs. Mitchell's oven," said Julie as she left.

She was trying to decide what to say first, when Mrs. Mitchell looked up and saw her coming.

"Hello, dahling," she called out, leaning on her broom, waiting for Julie to reach her.

"Hello," Julie said, wondering how soon she could get to the subject of cats.

With the clairvoyance of a witch, Mrs. Mitchell said, "Is there anything I can do for you, dahling?"

That makes it easy, thought Julie. But instead she found it hard to go on. The eyes looked small and black and impenetrable, the face blotched with red veins, the teeth revealed by a smile, yellow and sharp.

And she thought Mrs. Mitchell smelled of bubbling cauldrons with dead bats in them. She wanted to get away.

"Would you like a little card with the Twenty-third Psalm on it?" Mrs. Mitchell asked.

Julie didn't know what to say. If she took the card from Mrs. Mitchell, would Mrs. Mitchell reciprocate by taking the cat from her?

"You know how it starts, don't you, dahling? 'The Lord is my shepherd, I shall not want, he leadeth—' "

"Would you save my cat?" asked Julie.

Mrs. Mitchell looked at her for a minute. "If it's yours," she said, "why does it need saving?"

"It isn't really mine," said Julie. "It's a stray cat, and Cal and I have been feeding it and my parents say it's a nuisance. I mean that's its name. But it isn't really a nuisance." Julie knew by the confused look on Mrs. Mitchell's face that she had stopped making sense. "It's a very nice, friendly stray cat," she said. "And they might send it to the county. They say that something has to be done about it soon."

"I'm sorry, dahling." Mrs. Mitchell took her cane off of her arm and leaned on it with one hand, holding onto the broom with the other. "I'm too old and sick to take care of a cat," she said. "Sometimes I stay in bed all day. And I get so cold. The doctor says it's my heart."

"I understand," said Julie. What else could she say? She tried not to sound as disappointed as she felt.

"You've asked your friends," Mrs. Mitchell said.

"Most of them," said Julie. "I don't have very many." She didn't want to become too self-pitying.

How was she going to make her wish come true if she wasted time feeling sorry for herself? "We haven't lived here long," she explained.

"Do you want the card?" Mrs. Mitchell asked.

What card? Julie was startled. Even if Mrs. Mitchell couldn't help, Julie expected her to spend a few minutes being sympathetic. I might have known, Julie thought bitterly, she's forgotten already. Anyhow, witches probably don't take good care of their cats. Nuisance would probably never get fed and would have to ride on broomsticks. Julie could have laughed at the thought, if it weren't that she felt more like crying. But she would have been better than the county, Julie thought to herself despondently. Then she remembered the card. "The Lord is my shepherd . . . ."

"Sure," said Julie. I guess she still wants to do something for me, she thought, so I'd better let her. When you can't get out much and then you can only walk with a cane, it's probably hard to find things to do for other people.

"Come along and I'll fetch it for you," Mrs. Mitchell said.

"All right," said Julie. She followed Mrs. Mitchell up the path, up the steps, across the porch, and into the house.

At first Julie couldn't see anything, the front hall was so dark. However, once she got used to peering about in the dark rooms where all the curtains were shut, she found the inside of the house more tolerable than she had expected. Even the closed-up, basement odors didn't overwhelm her as she had feared they would.

It's perfect for ghosts, Julie thought. They probably flourish in dark, damp places just the way mushrooms do.

Now that she had lured an audience into her house, Mrs. Mitchell took Julie on a tour of all the objects of interest. "Those are my eighty-four birthday cards," she said, pointing into the dining room where the table and buffet were covered with cards standing up on display.

Once Mrs. Mitchell started talking, she flowed from one subject to the next and one object to the next without leaving any breathing spaces in between. Julie thought alternately, Why doesn't she give me the card and let me go? and, Why not stay? What else is there for me to do? As long as I can't think of anyone else to ask about Nuisance, I might as well be here.

"This is Len's cello," Mrs. Mitchell was saying, "and here's our wedding picture, and here's a picture of Len's parents, and that clock on the mantel is so heavy it takes three men to carry it, and here's a picture of Len's school, and here he is with the boys in the class. He was such a good man."

"Who's that?" Julie asked. Even though she wanted to get away, she felt she should seem interested. It was a picture of a woman with an intelligent, lively face, wearing a mortarboard and an academic gown and holding a diploma.

"Oh, that's the day I graduated from law school," said Mrs. Mitchell.

"You did!" said Julie. She couldn't keep from sounding surprised.

"Yes, I did," Mrs. Mitchell said with pride. "I never

practiced law, though. Len didn't want me to." Len, Len's parents—death and romance—so much living was recorded in that one room. All those ghosts! Perhaps Mrs. Mitchell kept the rooms dark so the ghosts would be happy there. As Julie stood half-listening to Mrs. Mitchell's reminiscences, worrying about taking control of her own life by finding a home for a stray cat, she had a soothing awareness of space and distance, of the grand sweep of all human life.

Mrs. Mitchell kept on talking, talking. If she were ever going to leave, Julie knew she would have to interrupt. "My mom will be wondering where I am," she said.

"Of course," said Mrs. Mitchell. "We can't worry your pretty mother." She produced a card from a little rack by the front door. "Here you are, dahling. Read it before you go to bed."

"I will," said Julie, putting it in her jacket pocket along with an old tissue and the key to the house. "Thank you."

"Come again, dahling," said Mrs. Mitchell as she closed the front door behind her. "You know, I just love people." That was all she said. She seemed to have forgotten about the cat.

Julie stood on the porch blinking. It was a relief to be out where everything was bright and fresh. She turned and looked at the picture of the shepherd holding the lamb. "If you were here," Julie whispered, "you could do it. But it's too hard for her to help."

When she got back to the house, Nuisance was there, waiting with an impatience borne of trust. "You dear thing," she said, sitting down on the back step and lifting Nuisance onto her lap. "I promise you, I'm not going to give up." Brave words, but she had really run out of ideas.

After sitting in her lap long enough to allow a few strokes, Nuisance jumped down and turned around as if to say, Well, where is it?

"You are a greedy puss," said Julie. "I'm giving you affection and all you want is food."

Julie poured one bowl of milk and then a second. "If you want more," she said, "go ask Cal. I'm sure he'll give you some tuna fish."

Nuisance sat on the bricks where they were still warm from the sun and started a thorough washing.

"Don't forget to wash your nose," reminded Julie, watching the busy pink tongue. "I'm not going to give up," she said again. Nuisance came over and put both paws on her knee as if to say, "Thank you." Then Julie started to stroke Nuisance and Nuisance settled down in her lap for a time of purring.

They only said soon, Julie thought. That could be any time. Even next week. But that might be too long for Stephen to wait. By then, the pine siskin might be scared away for good.

If I can have one more day, Julie thought. I'll ask Mrs. Barker and Wilma and Arnold Finch. It's hard asking people and being turned down. And they all have good reasons. But I'll keep trying.

The sun had almost set and it was getting cold. As Julie stood up, Nuisance slid to the ground. "I'd better go in," she said. "No, you can't come." As usual, Nuisance tried to follow her. "Oh, Nuisance, I want so badly to find a home for you."

When her mother got back, Julie helped make hamburger patties and cook the string beans. She also set the table. Nothing was said about the cat until the end of dinner, when Julie was finishing the last section of her tangerine. Then that special signal was passed between Mom and Stephen that meant, It's time for a talk.

"Julie," said her mother. "We've got to take some action about the cat."

Here it comes, thought Julie. The usual. When I get told what's going to happen.

"It can't live on what we've been feeding it," said Stephen.

"And it is having a discouraging effect on the birds," said her mother.

"I'm sorry, Julie," said Stephen, "but I feel so strongly that birds need to be protected from cats."

"We wanted to ask you—" said her mother.

Darn that telephone! Mom and Stephen were about to ask her something. And she was going to have a chance to say what she thought about Nuisance. They might answer their own question before the phone call was over.

"I'll get it," she said, knocking some tangerine skin off the plate in her haste. Maybe she could tell whoever it was to call later.

She let the kitchen door swing closed behind her and reached for the receiver. "Hello," she said.

"Hello, dahling." Only Mrs. Mitchell could sound like a creaking door.

"Hello," said Julie a second time.

"Don't forget to read it before you go to bed," said Mrs. Mitchell.

"I won't," said Julie and sighed. What a crazy old woman! To think Julie had gone to her for help!

"Is your cat still there?" Mrs. Mitchell asked.

"Yes," said Julie. It was too much. She tried to think of a way to end the conversation quickly.

"You know my friend," and Mrs. Mitchell started in on a long digression about the lady in the black Cadillac. "You remember her?"

"Yes," said Julie impatiently, "yes." Of course she remembered her from the time Cal fell off his bike—chirrupy and bright, a very comforting person.

"You do still have it?" Mrs. Mitchell asked.

"What?" said Julie.

"The cat for her grandson."

"The cat? You mean Nuisance?" said Julie.

"No, I mean the cat," said Mrs. Mitchell.

Julie started laughing. It was all so ridiculous. It was so wonderful. Mrs. Mitchell with her cane and her rolled-down stockings was going to be the shepherd after all.

"Is eight o'clock too early? She's driving to Richmond to see him tomorrow."

"I'll ask my mom," said Julie, "and I'll call you back right away. It'll only be a minute." Suppose Mrs. Mitchell didn't understand her? "I'll call you back in a minute."

"You'd better take my number," said Mrs. Mitchell. She did understand. "429-0077." It was a magic number.

"I'll call you right back," Julie said.

Mom and Stephen looked at her questioningly when she returned to the dinner table. Julie noticed how quickly their heads turned toward her. They really worry about me, she thought, the way I worry about Nuisance.

"It was Mrs. Mitchell," she said, looking back at them both. Stephen was frowning. His eyes seemed dark and tired.

"What did she want?" her mother asked. Maybe his eyes would become brighter when she told them about Mrs. Mitchell. Maybe he would look happy again, the way he had when he rescued her the night before.

"I asked her whether she would take the cat," Julie explained.

Stephen half-smiled. "That was brave of you, Julie. I find her intimidating."

"So do I. But after the robbery, she said she wanted to help me."

"I doubt whether she can manage a cat," her mother said.

"I'm afraid it would be back on our doorstep in two days," Stephen added. "It was a good idea. She might be lonely. But it wouldn't work." He was very definite.

"But we want to know what Julie thinks." Mom seemed to be reminding him and herself. "That's what we wanted to ask you . . . ." she persisted.

"You don't need to ask me." Julie finally found a chance to continue. "It's all worked out." She was going to surprise them after all.

"Not with Mrs. Mitchell?" said her mother.

"How?" said Stephen.

"Mrs. Mitchell has a friend with a grandson in Richmond. She wants to take the cat to him when she goes tomorrow morning. Is that all right?"

There was an amazed silence. Julie could almost

have laughed aloud. Mom and Stephen were prepared for a long, calm discussion about what to do with the cat, and now it was unnecessary.

"Is it all right?" she said again.

"Of course it is," said Stephen decisively. "It's the perfect solution."

"As long as . . . ." Mom didn't seem to know how to continue. "You don't feel too bad, do you, Julie?"

"No," said Julie. "It happened the way I wanted it to."

"That's good of you to say." Mom nodded in appreciation.

"I mean it, Mom," said Julie, because she did. They both looked toward Stephen. He was smiling.

"Thanks, Julie," he said. "You managed it very well. How many people did you ask?"

"Lots," she said, "starting with my dad." Something had happened. She could even talk about her real father with Stephen.

"Your dad did mention," said Mom, "that you were worried about a cat."

So that was it! They had understood the message of the visit to her father. That's what they were telling her. That they were ready to listen to her ideas about what should be done with Nuisance. Which meant that they cared. When people listened to you, you could tell they cared about you and wanted you with them. Which meant she wasn't a nuisance anymore.

"How do you want to arrange things?" Stephen asked. He waited while Julie thought about her answer.

"I'm going to call Mrs. Mitchell, and then I'm going

to find the cat and keep it on the porch tonight, if that's all right."

Julie went out to the kitchen and dialed Mrs. Mitchell's number. "I'll be there with the cat tomorrow morning," she said. "Thank you. You're so kind."

"Remember, read it tonight, dahling," Mrs. Mitchell said before she hung up.

Then Julie put on her heavy jacket and went to look for Nuisance. Actually, there was no way she could find Nuisance in the dark. She could only hope that hearing her there, Nuisance would come to her for more milk.

"Nuisance," she called. "Nuisance." No cat. It wasn't the end yet. Not until she had delivered the cat to Mrs. Mitchell's house could she say that her wish had come true. "Nuisance!" Was the plan going to fail because she couldn't find Nuisance?

Julie walked down the driveway toward the street. If Nuisance wasn't at her house . . . . She looked over toward Cal's porch. The light was on and Cal, wearing a heavy white sweater, was standing under it, holding Nuisance in his arms—Like a Shepherd.

"Cal!" Julie ran over to him. "That's so lucky. I got my wish. I made it happen, the way you told me to. And now you have the cat. Just when I need it."

"Was it the gloves, Jewel?" asked Cal, handing Nuisance to her. "Or the witch?"

"Mainly the witch," said Julie. "I took your advice and asked." And with Nuisance purring sleepily in her arms, she told Cal about her visit to Mrs. Mitchell.

While they talked, Nuisance woke up and started to wiggle. "I think I'd better go," said Julie. "Before Nuisance tries to escape."

Cal put his hand on top of Julie's as it held the cat. It seemed to calm Nuisance. "Good night, Princess Jewel," he said. "I'm glad you were strong enough to save the royal cat, even if you had to make friends with a witch to do it." He held onto her hand for a minute with his own, which seemed so much larger, and then said, "See you tomorrow."

Nuisance stayed relaxed in her arms until Julie reached the back porch. She locked the porch door and held the cat against her cheek.

"Good night, Nuisance," she said. "You're going where someone wants you. And then you'll have a new name. You won't be a nuisance anymore."

About The Author

Fredericka Berger graduated from Swarthmore College and the Harvard School of Education. She has taught junior and senior high-school English in Boston and Philadelphia, and has written and directed plays for church groups in the Washington area where she lives with her husband and two sons. This is her first novel.